THE GAY DOGS

Being the Further Adventures of

That Man from C.A.M.P.

by

Victor J. Banis

The Borgo Press
An Imprint of Wildside Press

MMVII

SECOND EDITION

♠ CONTENTS ♠
λ

♠ FOREWORD ♠
TO THE SECOND EDITION
λ

The books in the series, *The Man from C.A.M.P.*, were among the earliest of the many novels I have penned. They were written in the 1960s, and they are very much a part of that exciting era when people of so many different sorts were coming out of so many different closets. Gay people were celebrating in the streets the very same lifestyle that only a few years before had engendered in many of us guilt and shame and fear, ruined large numbers of promising careers and sent many to prison.

These books were a part of my celebration. They were written with tongue very firmly in cheek, in a few days each, with nary a thought of rewrite or polishing up some admittedly amateurish prose. They were never intended to be "literature," and they are not. They were, however, intended to be fun.

I think they still are.

—Victor J. Banis
July 2006

♠ THE MAN FROM C.A.M.P. ♠
CHECKLIST
λ

1. *The Man from C.A.M.P.*
2. **Color Him Gay*
3. *The Watercress File*
4. *The Son Goes Down*
5. *Gothic Gaye*
6. *Holiday Gay*
7. *Rally Round the Fag*
8. **The Gay Dogs*
9. *Blow the Man Down*
10. *Gay-Safe* (not written by Victor Banis)

*=Published by Wildside Press

Associated Titles:

Sex and the Single Gay
The C.A.M.P. Guide to Astrology
The C.A.M.P. Cookbook

♠ CHAPTER ONE ♠
λ

Jackie Holmes smiled slightly to himself as he felt a warm pressure against his right leg. He did not have to turn in that direction to know who was sitting on that side of him at the bar. He had already cast plenty of glances in that direction.

Necessary or not, however, he did glance after all. He started down, at the leg pressing lightly against his. A nice leg, thick and muscular, and encased in faded Levi's that fit like a second skin. His eyes moved slowly upward, to the round smoothness of a thigh, across the lap, unmarred by any "belly bulge." Not that there was an absence of bulges. They were there, certainly, in the right places between the thighs, and sizable enough to be impressive. Sufficiently impressive that Jackie didn't hurry about raising his eyes.

When he did raise them, they traveled up a small but muscular torso. He saw husky bare arms, pale in color and lightly marked with freckles and wispy, golden red hair. And broad shoulders, full with muscles.

The trip stopped at the face. "Cute" was the word that it called to mind. The sandy red hair above it didn't quite want to stay in place, and a few loose strands fell over the high forehead. Green eyes twinkled as they returned his look. The nose turned up, as though displaying with pride its array of freckles. The chin was dimpled, and the full mouth was stretched in a provocative grin.

"How did the inventory come out?" the stranger asked, his grin broadening.

"Most satisfactory," Jackie assured him, responding with a smile. He liked the voice, too: low, throaty, caressing. "Are you waiting for anyone?"

"Not just anyone," was the answer. The pressure on Jackie's leg increased slightly. And so did the pressure at the pit of Jackie's stomach.

It had started as a dull night for Jackie. The slender blond had found himself with a free evening: nothing and no one to do. The Westgate, a quiet little beer bar he sometimes visited, had seemed like a likely place to correct the situation. To his disappointment, however, the place had offered rather scant prospects.

He had been on the verge of finishing his beer and leaving when the redhead had entered and taken a seat next to him. The way things were progressing, it looked as though he would soon have something to do after all. Or someone.

It was at that moment that Lady Agatha entered the bar, pausing just inside the swinging door to adjust his eyes to the dim light. Jackie knew, as soon as he saw his gay friend, that his hopes for whisking his new playmate quickly away were in vain.

Lady Agatha was a close friend, of many years standing, and one whose company Jackie ordinarily enjoyed immensely, but he was not the sort of friend with whom one exchanged a fast hello and goodbye.

Lady Agatha liked to talk. His supply of gossip, anecdotes, news, and just plain trivia, was virtually endless, and always eagerly shared.

Having become accustomed to the lighting, Lady Agatha looked slowly around him. His eyes widened when he saw Jackie, and even more when they rested on the attractive young man seated beside Jackie. Lady Agatha greatly appreciated masculine beauty.

Jackie knew as he watched the smiling brunette cross the room, that he was in for competition.

"Hello, sweets," Agatha greeted him. His glance quickly and meaningfully moved on to Jackie's companion. "And what have we here? Someone I haven't met yet."

"To be honest, I haven't officially met him either," Jackie answered, realizing he still didn't know his new friend's name. He turned also to the redhead.

"I'm Don Daniels." Jackie's hand was clasped in a firm grip.

"Jackie Holmes. And this is my old friend, Al Barlow."

"Better known as Lady Agatha. And be careful about using words such as old." Lady Agatha shook hands with Don, her eyes making much the same trip Jackie's had made before, with a few side visits.

"How did you ever get a name such as Lady Agatha?" Don asked. "You don't look like a Lady Agatha to me."

"It's a long story," Jackie answered before Lady Agatha could start with an explanation. He knew from past experience that once Agatha got the conversational ball rolling, he would hang on to it until he had made a basket, and this time Jackie had his heart set on being the one who got the basket. "It had to do with a bar we used to frequent, called The Why Not. Some evening when we have lots of time, I'll tell you all about it."

"There's nothing wrong with the present," Agatha countered. "Unless someone's in a hurry."

Jackie suppressed a sigh of disappointment. His spirits lifted however as he looked up and his eyes met Don's. Unless he was a poor judge, Don was just as impatient to be going as he was.

"Well, as a matter of fact, we were just planning to finish our beers and leave," Jackie answered.

The conversation was interrupted temporarily by the arrival of the bartender, carrying two glasses of beer. "From an admirer," he explained, setting one in front of Don. "And one for you, from the same admirer," he finished, handing the other one to Lady Agatha.

"Who's our admiring friend?" Don asked.

"The fellow at the other end of the bar," the bartender explained, nodding toward the end where a single individual sat by himself. Both Don and Agatha smiled in the direction of their benefactor, and lifted their glasses in silent thanks.

"Heavens, men literally throwing themselves at my feet," Agatha exclaimed. "I suppose I should go down there and let him bask in my charm for a few moments."

"If you do that," Don answered. "I still won't get to hear your story, and as long as we have to stay to finish these beers, you might as well tell me all about that."

Jackie felt suddenly left out of the scene. It was not only a question of vanity. After all, there had been plenty of men to send him drinks before, and would be again. At the same time, it was puzzling that the stranger would have signaled out Agatha and Don for his attention and ignored a third person with them.

Unless, of course, he was interested in getting a three-way started. That wasn't as unusual as many people thought, particularly in a bar of this sort.

The really disappointing fact, however, was that Don's attention was now suddenly all centered on Agatha and her story. A moment before, Jackie had been sure Don's interest was in him. Now Don had eyes only for Agatha. Neither one of them, in fact, seemed to notice that Jackie was without a drink.

Silently, Jackie signaled the bartender to bring him another beer also, and turned to listen politely to Agatha's familiar narrative.

It was, as usual with Agatha, an entertaining bit of conversation. Despite his disappointment, Jackie found himself sharing Don's laughter. It was impossible to remain annoyed with Agatha for more than a few moments.

By the time they had nearly finished their beers, Jackie was once again in good spirits. Now that the conversational scene was ending, he was confident he and Don would be leaving together.

"Heavens, I've been talking so much I scarcely knew I'd finished my beer," Agatha declared. He glanced from one to the other, and then remembering his manners, gave Jackie's leg a pat. "But I know you two were anxious to be on your way. I'll let you make your escape now."

"Don't be silly," Don objected. "I'm having a great time."

Taking no notice of Jackie's surprise and consternation, Don signaled the bartender for three more beers. Glumly, Jackie resigned himself to further delays. It was beginning to look like Agatha would be winning the prize after all, without even really trying.

The conversation continued through the next beer, with Agatha as usual doing most of the talking, and Don an enthusiastic audience. Jackie kept up an appearance of interest, even though his heart wasn't really in it. He glanced once around the bar, wondering if there was anything else present that he should be working on, just in case.

He saw the stranger who had sent the beers to Agatha and Don. Not bad, Jackie decided, studying the man briefly. A little too beefy and husky for Jackie's taste—not the type one would want to meet in a dark alley—and not the type, Jackie found himself thinking, you would expect to send drinks to strangers in bars.

Now that's just sour grapes, he told himself angrily. It was nothing short of childish to resent the fact that his two companions had been singled out for some flattery.

12

The stranger got up and made his way toward the door out of the bar. He caught Agatha's eye as he went, and called a friendly, "Good night."

"Oh, you're not leaving?" Agatha interrupted herself. "Won't you join us and let us repay the beer?"

"Afraid not," the stranger answered. "I've got an engagement already." He gave Don a wave also, and disappeared through the door.

"Peculiar one," Agatha decided, staring after him. "I was sure he was positively smitten by me. Or by the both of us, I should say.

"Maybe he decided you were inseparable," Jackie commented.

"I guess we'd better be going," Don declared, finishing off the last of the beer. It was an abrupt change of interest that caught Jackie off guard.

"Fine," Jackie agreed with genuine enthusiasm.

"Oh, no you don't," Agatha said firmly. "Not until I've bought a round. After that, I'll leave you to yourselves." He placed some money on the bar. "Be a dear and get them for me, Jackie. I have to go out to the car and check on Cynthia."

"Cynthia?" Don asked, puzzled.

"A Yorkshire terrier," Jackie explained. "But you don't mean to tell me she's been outside all this time?"

"Oh, pooh" Agatha dismissed the note of concern with a wave of his hand. "She hasn't been suffering, I can assure you. Once she's eaten, she sleeps like a dead person. She probably doesn't even know I'm not in the car with her. Anyway the doors are all locked, so she's plenty safe."

Agatha headed out of the bar, while Jackie shrugged and gave Don a weak smile. "I guess we'll have to have one more," he said. "But we can drink them fast."

"Fine."

Curious, Jackie found himself thinking, *a very puzzling young man*. Even though it was Don who had finally suggested they leave, Jackie could not quite get over the feeling that the redhead really did not much care whether they went together or not. Jackie dismissed the thought, however, and ordered the drinks.

Agatha was back in a moment, and it was obvious from the instant that he burst through the door that something was wrong. There was alarm written all over his face, and as he rushed across the small room toward Jackie, there were tears in his eyes. "Jackie, something awful has happened," he exclaimed. "They've taken my baby, Cynthia"

"Cynthia?" Jackie jumped to his feet. "Who's taken her?"

"I don't know," Agatha wailed, fairly beside himself. "She's been stolen. Oh, come see, please."

Jackie was out of the door before Agatha. He looked down the darkened side street and recognized Agatha's car at once, a small lavender economy Chevelle. Even before he reached the car, he could see the smashed windows and. the brick lying nearby that had been used to smash them. Someone had wanted inside the car very badly. Even on a dark side street, they were taking a terrific chance of being caught.

"You see, they've stolen her right out of the car," Agatha cried, running up to join him. "Oh, what am I going to do? What a cruel thing."

Jackie reached through the window and opened the locked door. His eyes darted about the car's interior. On the back seat was a suede jacket, Agatha's. Attached to the dashboard was a flashlight. The car hadn't been emptied, or stripped. It had been the dog, and only the dog, they had been after.

"Better call the police," Jackie said. "Call from the bar."

"The police?" It was Don who said this, walking up at a more leisurely pace to join them. "Isn't that a little drastic?"

"So was this," Jackie reminded him sharply.

"But that's a gay bar," Don argued.

"So what?" Jackie forgot his attraction for the redhead in his annoyance. "Why should homosexuals forfeit all rights and privileges because they're afraid of the police? This is a theft, and a dastardly act. It's a police matter."

"Couldn't you handle it?" Agatha asked in an anxious voice.

Jackie shot him a warning glance. "I'm hardly qualified to do the work of the police for them."

Agatha caught the glance, and remembered Don's presence. "I guess you're right," he admitted. "Oh, my poor Cynthia. You don't suppose they'll treat her badly, do you?"

"Obviously they recognized her for a valuable dog," Jackie assured his friend, steering him back toward the bar. "I'm sure they'll treat her accordingly."

Secretly he was less confident. He had read accounts of dogs being stolen, and sold to universities and colleges for laboratory work. But he could not imagine going to so much trouble to steal prize dogs for that purpose, when a mongrel off the streets would be just as valuable.

The bartender was sympathetic when he heard the news, and although the necessity of calling the police into the bar was obviously unpleasant for him, he offered no objections. There was only one other customer in the bar by this time. Jackie made a point of warning the stranger what bad happened, and that the police had been called. He too was sympathetic, and agreed nervously to stay.

There was not much, however, that the police could do. They examined the car, checking for fingerprints, and talked to each of the people in the bar. No one could shed any clues. No sounds had been heard, nor did a brief check of the mostly industrial neighborhood reveal any witnesses.

"We'll make a report," the officer said finally to Agatha. "And we'll let you know when we learn anything."

"Do you think I'll get her back?" Agatha asked.

The officer shrugged. "Hard to say."

The officers left, leaving a dispirited group behind.

"Come on," Jackie said, dropping a comforting arm around Agatha's shoulders. "I'll follow you home, and have a drink with you there." He turned to Don. "I hope you'll understand, and let me have a rain check."

"Sure," Don replied. "I'll give you my phone number, and maybe we can get together a little later in the week."

The three of them exchanged telephone numbers. Jackie was grateful that Don was being so gracious about everything. He watched as the redhead left alone, his tightly encased buttocks bouncing slightly as he walked away. Jackie promised himself that he would make use of the phone number, but for tonight, he had Agatha to think of. His friend's needs came first, and he had no regrets. He knew that, in a similar situation, Agatha would do the same.

"Would you rather leave your car here?" Jackie asked as they left the bar. "I can drive you home."

"I suppose there's little point in worrying about its being broken into," Agatha agreed glumly. "I'll get my jacket."

Jackie waited patiently as Agatha went to fetch the jacket. He could understand how badly Agatha felt. He himself had a dog to whom he was terribly attached. He imagined how badly he would feel if anything happened to Sophie, his miniature white poodle.

Except, of course, the same thing would not be likely to happen to Sophie. Had it been Sophie the thieves had attempted to steal, they would have found themselves in a bit of trouble. Trouble, after all, was a specialty with Sophie.

Trouble was a specialty with Jackie, also. In the bar, and in the presence of strangers, Jackie kept up an appearance of frivolity and helplessness. He was slender and small, with a pretty face and a slightly effeminate manner. But beneath this seemingly harmless exterior he played another role, one in striking contrast. The slender body that appeared frail and helpless was in fact one of wiry and incredible strength, kept in perfect shape by an almost superhuman program of exercise. In the hidden area that he utilized for his workouts, Jackie had performed athletic feats that, if he chose to display them publicly, would make him famous in the sports world. He had run the mile in nearly a half minute less than the world record. In jumping, vaulting, lifting, swimming, his achievements were considerably better than what was publicly regarded as the best.

His sometimes scatterbrained mentality was a fake too. His mind was keen and alert at all times, and possessing knowledge equal to the great minds of the world.

On the surface, Jackie appeared to be an ordinary, insignificant homosexual. In fact, he was a highly regarded secret agent for an organization unknown to most individuals, an organization dedicated to the advancement and protection of homosexuals throughout the world.

Jackie Holmes was the Man from C.A.M.P.

♠ CHAPTER TWO ♠
λ

"Isn't there anything your organization can do?" Agatha asked as Jackie drove swiftly and skillfully through the Los Angeles traffic. Jackie's identity as the Man from C.A.M.P. was no secret to Agatha.

"I don't know," Jackie answered honestly. "If anything comes up, of course, I'll personally do all I can to help. But there doesn't seem to be any particular connection with homosexuality. Your proclivities and the fact that the robbery took place while you were in a gay bar, may be nothing more than coincidence."

"But it's such an awful crime," Agatha argued. "Who would stoop so low as to steal a helpless animal? People like that should be brought to justice."

"I agree. And I promise you to see what I can do—although, frankly, without any clues, I don't know just what can be done."

They were pulling up outside the apartment house in which Agatha lived. "I'll be all right,"

Agatha said, giving Jackie's hand a pat. "There's no need for you to come up. I'd rather you see what you can do to find Cynthia for me."

"I'll do what I can. In the meantime, the police have been called in also. If they come up with anything, work along with them, too."

Alone in the car, Jackie drove rapidly, to another part of the city. The street on which he finally found himself was cheap and tawdry. Jackie parked at the curb and made his way to the entrance of a bar, where a faded sign labeled the place as the Round Up. The Round Up was a gay bar, but not the sort likely to be included on any out-of-town visitor's tour. The lights were dim, but not so dim that they concealed the rundown condition of the place: a battered counter, torn plastic hanging loose from the stools, debris generously mixed with the sawdust on the floor.

This evening the place was nearly empty. The bartender scarcely looked up from the newspaper he was reading, and the two lone customers at the bar seemed not to have noticed that Jackie had entered. Jackie was not a typical customer of the Round Up, but he had been seen entering the door often enough that no one questioned his appearance now.

Without a pause, Jackie made his way to the rear. A curtained doorway opened into a narrow hall with doors to the restrooms. Jackie entered the one marked "MEN" and paused inside the door.

The room was empty. He passed by the urinals, badly in need of cleaning, and made his way to the twin stalls at the far end of the room. One of them was marked with an OUT OF ORDER sign. Ignoring this, Jackie stepped inside and lifted the ceramic top of the water closet, plunging his hand inside. He felt about for a moment, until he found the switch.

With a click and a whir of gears, the end wall swung open. Jackie stepped through the opening, plunged into momentary darkness as the door closed. Then another door opened before him into a lighted room.

It was like stepping into another world. From the seedy bar, Jackie had entered a spacious and luxurious apartment. Flickering candles and gleaming crystal cast myriad lights and shadows upon the walls that were covered with velvet. In the immense fireplace the inevitable fire was burning low.

As Jackie entered the apartment, a man entered the same room through another door. He flashed a pleased smile as Jackie came into the room.

"Hi, Rich," Jackie greeted his partner in C.A.M.P. "How about a drink?"

At Rich's affirmative nod, Jackie poured cognac for them from the crystal decanter on the table. Unlike Jackie, Rich was the sort who would probably never be recognized for a homosexual. Rich stood six foot five inches, handsome in a dark, rugged way. Despite his football-player build, though, and his massive proportions, he moved with a lithe, animal grace that belied his great strength.

"What's up?" Rich asked, accepting the brandy.

"Just a small incident. Small but unpleasant." Briefly, Jackie explained about the theft of Agatha's dog. Rich listened silently and attentively. To the more than casual observer, his eyes revealed that the man's mind was as strong as his body.

"Interesting," Rich agreed when the story was finished. "As you say, it may involve a lot of coincidence, or it may be a lead to something big. Dognapping is becoming more and more common, these days. Not too long ago, if you recall, the police uncovered a large dognapping ring."

"Yes, I recall that. This may be something equally large, or even larger. Of course, it'll have to be cleared with High Camp, and then there's still the question of where does one start."

"We can start with the files," Rich suggested. "C.A.M.P.'s files should give us all the information on every reported dognapping over the last year. It should be easy enough to determine if there's a pattern."

"Good idea," Jackie said, "Let's see what we can find."

Rich disappeared through a doorway into the inner recesses of this C.A.M.P. office. Here was kept the highly complex equipment, which assisted in the operations of C.A.M.P. Complete files, on microfilm, contained information on literally millions of homosexuals and homosexual activities throughout the world. There were files too on criminals throughout the world, many of them literally unknown to the police, criminals whose activities effected in some way the homosexual world.

Through this office, as well, Rich was in constant communication with the ultra secret headquarters of the operation, High Camp. Few of C.A.M.P.'s personnel knew the location of High Camp, for nearly all of them worked out of local offices such as this one. But they all knew the far-reaching authority and capabilities, of High Camp.

Crime was not the only field in which C.A.M.P worked. There were special sections that dealt with law, with social problems, with health and psychiatry, and with science. The laboratories of C.A.M.P were superior to any others, complete with equipment yet unknown to the outside world. Whatever information, equipment, or assistance an agent might need in solving a case, High Camp was sure to have it.

It was the job of Rich, and the others like him, to serve as the link between the agents, such as Jackie, and High Camp itself.

Rich was back in a surprisingly short time, carrying a paper on which he had made some brief notes.

"Well, it may be something," he said, glancing over his notes. "Eighteen dognappings in the last three months. Ten of them have had homosexual implications; dogs stolen while their owners were in gay bars, or the owners were obviously homosexual. All of them, by the way, have been valuable dogs, some of them prizewinners."

"It might be a lead," Jackie agreed thoughtfully. "As we both know, unscrupulous people will often prey on the homosexual because they know that many homosexuals regard themselves as outside the law, and therefore no action will be taken by the victims."

"It's an unfortunate situation," Rich said. "So long as the laws regarding homosexuality remain in effect, the homosexual lives as a man without legal rights, because by his very nature, he's a criminal."

"And crime will continue to flourish, at the

expense of the homosexual," Jackie added. "Who knows how many blackmailers, hoods, murderers and thieves are free to practice their crimes to their hearts' content, thanks to a tragic lack of justice."

"Someday," Rich said fervently, "C.A.M.P. will achieve the ultimate goal of returning his legal and human rights to the homosexual. Thank Heaven there is at least C.A.M.P. to fight for that goal.

"I'll hang on to these notes," Jackie decided grimly. "And just as a matter of curiosity, I may try contacting some of these people, If this is organized crime, directed at the homosexual, it's up to us to bring it to an end."

He stood, downing the last of his cognac. "Guess I'd better call it a night."

Rich was standing too, near him. His dark eyes stared down into Jackie's, and his lips parted in a smile. "You don't have to rush out, you know."

Jackie looked up into the ruggedly chiseled face, returning the smile. "Am I being propositioned?"

"You know how I feel about you."

Jackie lifted a finger to Rich's lips. "Yes, I know. We've discussed it often. But we both know that it can never be all the way with us. Occasionally a few stolen moments together, but that's all we can ever have. Our work is our lives. It has to be that way."

"I know," Rich said with an unhappy sigh.

Jackie softened. Although his feelings were not as deep as those of Rich, he did feel a great deal of affection for his companion. He knew, too, how exciting a few stolen moments could be with Rich, and excitement meant a great deal to Jackie.

"We could spare some time tonight, though," he said aloud. "If you want."

Rich's face brightened immediately. "Do I?" he declared. "What do you think?"

Jackie followed his glance downward. Even in a normal state, Rich's endowments could not help but be conspicuous. They were even more so now, straining mightily against the fabric of his trousers. As often as he had seen the sight, and even enjoyed the pleasures that it offered, Jackie could not help but be thrilled. He felt his own body stirring with desires.

He grinned broadly, and without another word stepped past Rich and headed toward the door that led to an elaborate bedroom beyond. The lights here were a dim red, creating an eerie, almost otherworldly effect. The bed was vast, a veritable playground of soft mattresses and silk sheets.

Jackie undressed quickly, eager to take advantage of the opportunity that was afforded them. The body that he revealed as he removed his clothing was a contradiction to the appearance he offered dressed. He had discarded his effeminate mannerisms, the pose that he wore for the benefit of others. Now, as he discarded his clothes as well, his body even seemed less slender than before. Beneath the surface of the gleaming skin, perfectly toned muscles rippled and danced. It was a young man's body, one that seemed created solely to provide pleasure, and one that was highly skilled in that art.

Reclining naked on the bed, Jackie watched as Rich finished undressing. His upper body was bare by now, a study in male magnificence. The massive chest was fringed with a pattern of the same dark hair that fell across, his forehead. His arms were hugely muscled, his shoulders the equal of Atlas.

Rich slipped out of his trousers, flattered and yet faintly embarrassed by the sigh of appreciation that came from the bed. The trail of dark hair led from his navel downward, across a hard, flat abdomen, blossoming out suddenly to frame the awesome male adornments that were now in full view.

Sexually, Rich was a giant, and the mere sight of his naked body had been sufficient to discourage many would-be playmates. Jackie knew from experience, however, that this was an instrument of pleasure, not unhappiness, used with the skill that separates the artist from the stud.

Rich came quickly to the bed. Jackie was swept up into the powerful arms, his lips crushed beneath those above him. His body seemed to fuse with the splendid figure of his partner.

The lips moved, after an eternity, from his, moving gently but eagerly downward. As the mouth explored Jackie's body, the hands moved skillfully from one spot to another, skillfully playing upon the most sensitive areas of the body, arousing Jackie to fever pitch.

Jackie gasped as the mouth reached its goal, teasing him for an agonizing moment before white-hot lips engulfed him. Instinctively, Jackie's hips moved, driving upward. Jackie opened his eyes and saw almost before his face the tower of pleasure he had admired a moment earlier. Without hesitation, he moved toward it, grasping it in his hands. Rich groaned as Jackie's lips devoured him, slowly and cautiously at first, then with excited determination.

There was no time for the little niceties which both enjoyed. They could not know how many minutes, perhaps only seconds, they would have for the act. Together, they gave themselves up to their passion, their bodies moving wildly in unison, a dance of lust.

Upward they soared, bodies crashing and thrusting, the violent slap of flesh against flesh punctuating each of their movements. Jackie felt as though he could not endure any more of this delicious agony he was experiencing. Surely his body must burst into a million pieces. He felt the signaling surge in Rich's flesh, and knew that they were still together, rushing wildly and simultaneously to the peak, the climax of their maddening orgy of flesh and desire.

They erupted together in a white hot crescendo, clawing and gasping breathlessly as they offered to one another the proof positive of their pleasure, the truly ultimate tribute to their ardor.

It had ended none too soon, as it were. Even as they fell apart on the bed, both panting mightily from their exertion, there was a faint tinkling sound in the room, much like the sound of glass wind chimes, except that there was no breeze in the room.

It was the signal from High Camp, calling Rich back to his post and his duties.

Rich smiled as he jumped quickly up from the bed and slipped into a silk robe hanging nearby. "Good thing we didn't waste any time," he commented. "I don't think I could have interrupted that while it was in progress."

As Rich left the room, Jackie also got up from the bed, and went into the adjoining bathroom to shower and clean up. Interludes like this were pleasant, but he and Rich had a great deal more to do.

Rich returned as Jackie was dressing again. "Anything exciting?" Jackie asked as Rich entered the room.

"Just routine, but unfortunately it will keep me busy for a few hours. Unfortunately, because I was just in the mood for a few repeats."

Jackie smiled and stretched up on his toes to kiss Rich lightly. "There'll always be next time. I'll pick up the leftovers then. For now, I'd better be on my way. There's work to be done, friend."

He made his way through the living room of the apartment, to its secret entrance. There he paused for a brief moment in the darkened space between the two doors, and opened a concealed panel on one wall. From here he could see into a tiny cubicle, where a man in a nondescript gray suit stood.

Jackie knew that the man was a policeman, and that the window through which the policeman was staring afforded a view into the adjoining restroom. From here, the policeman could watch for any homosexual activities, and initiate arrests.

Of course, the policemen who were constantly on duty there knew nothing of C.A.M.P.'s offices, or of the peephole through which Jackie now peered. It was a joke with Jackie, watching the watchmen. With a smile, he noticed that this particular watchman was quite attractive. Too bad, he thought as he continued on his way through the exit, that they were on opposite sides of the fence.

Emerging into the restroom, Jackie observed that it was empty. He stooped, so that he would be below the line of the vision of the watching policeman, and made his way from the restroom, and the bar, again without notice.

As he clambered into his car, his thoughts were already far from the policeman he had been admiring, and even from Rich and their torrid session of lovemaking that had taken place minutes before. He was thinking of Agatha and her stolen dog, Cynthia.

Was there a dognapping ring at work, preying upon those who were defenseless, such as homosexuals? If this was the case, how could he go about getting a lead on them?

Like all criminal groups, the dognapping ring if it existed, was certain to have a weakness somewhere in its structure, a flaw that would spell success for him and failure for them. His job was to find that flaw.

* * * * * * *

Lady Agatha started when the phone rang. For a moment he was uncomfortably aware that something was wrong about the ring, then he. put his finger on what was wrong: there was no Cynthia to bark, as she always did when the bell sounded. The thought only added to his gloom. He moved dispiritedly toward the phone.

"Mr. Barlow?" The voice was an unfamiliar one, masculine and ruggedly pleasant.

"Speaking." Agatha mentally contemplated the possibilities of who might be calling. He thought of the one from the bar, the one Jackie had been with when Cynthia was stolen. Don, that was his name, but his voice had been softer and more pleasant. This one had a harsh sound to it.

You don't know me," the voice continued. "My name is Harris, Mark Harris. I'm calling about a dog."

"A dog?" Agatha's heart was in his throat.

"Yes. I found one last night wandering around on the street, a little Yorkshire. She had a tag, with the name A. Barlow, but there were several Barlows listed, so I'm not sure I have the right one."

"Oh, it's Cynthia, it must be," Agatha said, excited. "But on the street, you say, wandering? That can't be, she was stolen last night." He had forgotten all about the nametag on Cynthia's collar. Thank heaven for that, he told himself.

"I don't know anything about that. She was just roaming the streets when I found her. I thought she looked like a good dog, so I picked her up. When I saw the name tag—well, to be honest, I thought anyone who owned a dog as nice as this one would probably be very grateful to have her found."

"Oh, I am," Agatha cried. "But where is she? When can I pick her up?"

"She's at my place." Mr. Harris was being hesitant.

"Oh." Agatha realized finally what he had meant by "grateful." "You mean a reward. But of course, it's worth anything to get her back. Would fifty dollars be all right?"

"Fine," Harris replied, much more cheerfully. "As a matter of fact, you can pick her up anytime. I'll be home this afternoon."

Agatha grabbed a pencil, and. wrote down the address, in the Silverlake area of the city. "I'll be there in about forty minutes," he promised.

Hastily he donned a sports coat, and grabbed his keys from the dresser. He was almost to the door when he thought of Jackie. Jackie would want to know. He started back toward the phone again, then caught himself. But that was silly, there was no crime involved in this. Whoever had stolen Cynthia had simply let her go, or perhaps Cynthia had somehow gotten away. Mr. Harris was just a nice man, maybe a little money hungry, but innocent of any crime. Agatha dismissed the idea of calling Jackie, and hurried from the door. Not until he was outside did he remember that his car was still parked by the Westgate.

He paused on the sidewalk in frustration. He could call a cab but he might have to wait fifteen or twenty minutes for the cab to arrive. There was a bus stop at the corner. Deciding on that course of action, he half ran, half walked to the bus stop.

Luck was with him this time. He caught a bus almost immediately. Within ten minutes he was at his car. He drove as fast as the law allowed in the direction of Silverlake.

It took a while to find the house. Silverlake was a neighborhood of hills and narrow, winding streets, some of them no more than a block or two long. He did find it, however: an old, rather large house, set back from the street and sitting rather isolated from its neighbors.

As he pulled into the drive, he heard a familiar bark, and looked up to the porch to see Cynthia jumping against the screen door. With a cry, he ran up the steps, rushing to the door.

So overjoyed was he at seeing Cynthia again

that he almost overlooked the man standing with her at the screen door. Agatha came to a stop just before he thoughtlessly threw open the door. After all, this was not his house.

"You must be Mr. Barlow," the stranger greeted him. "And I guess that's your dog all right. I'm Mark Harris."

Even in his excitement, Agatha could scarcely dismiss Mr. Harris lightly. H was a splendid example of manhood: tall, husky, almost painfully masculine. Tight Levi's left nothing to the imagination, and they were all that he wore, leaving a splendid upper torso bare.

"Yes, I'm Al Barlow, and I'm so grateful." Agatha allowed himself a flirtatious smile. Chances were Mr. Harris wasn't interested in anything but the monetary reward. Still, it never hurt to try. "If there's anything I can do...?"

"Come on in," Harris said, swinging the door open wide.

Cynthia jumped frantically into Agatha's arms. Dividing his attention between the attractive Mr. Harris and the jubilant Cynthia, Agatha stepped inside.

He stopped inside the door, his entire attention suddenly riveted elsewhere. The hallway in which he stood was separated from the large kitchen by a Dutch door, the upper half open. And the kitchen was literally filled with dogs, of all sorts— German Shepherds, poodles, terriers—all good breeds, too. They jumped at the door, some of them whining, some barking, some with their tails up and some with tails despondently down.

For the first time suspicion crept into

Agatha's mind. He began to wonder if Mr. Harris had really found Cynthia wandering on the streets.

"I see you're quite a dog fancier," he said aloud, trying to sound natural. If his suspicions were correct, then he was right in the den of the vipers who had stolen his Cynthia, and probably all those other dogs.

Harris shrugged without any sign of emotion. "You might say that. Come on back." He motioned for Agatha to make his way down the hall.

"Anna," he yelled down the hall. "We've got company. Mr. Barlow is here."

"Bring him back here," a feminine voice answered. "I'd like to meet him."

Agatha made his way with increasing reluctance down the hall, uncomfortably aware of the fact that the burly Mr. Harris was behind him. In his arms, Cynthia whined faintly, as though she too did not want to enter the room at the end of the hall.

The hall opened into a small, wood-paneled den. It might have been a cozy room, but the decor had been created to give anything but a "cozy" effect. The furnishings, low and modern, were all in leather and similar materials. A bench covered in black leather was trimmed in thick ropes. A leather light fixture was suspended on a black chain. The walls were covered with an alarming array of weapons and even instruments of torture: sabers, whips, maces. It was like something from the Inquisition.

Nor was the feminine occupant of the room likely to soften the impression. She was reclining on a leather sofa, and in her hands she hold a cat-o'-nine-tails, toying with it. The first impression one got of Anna was of a large jungle cat. Her black hair hung loosely about pale, bare shoulders. Her long, sleek body was covered only by a leather bikini, and she wore leather boots that came to her knees. She smiled as Agatha entered the room, but it was not a pleasant smile, more the sort a cat would smile as the mouse came into view.

"My boss," Harris said from behind. "Miss Lingus."

At the same time, another door from the den opened, and a third person joined them. Like Harris, this one was a breathtaking example of male animal beauty: dark, savage looking, with thin, menacing eyes and a brutally muscular body. Nor was it difficult to assess the body, for it was nearly nude. The newcomer, who was emerging from what apparently was a bathroom, wore nothing but a model's posing strap, a skimpy pouch which just managed to cover his bulging crotch, and in the process did nothing to conceal his build. From the pouch, nearly invisible threads encircled the hips, running down the crevice between the buttocks to pass between the thighs and attach to the bottom of the pouch.

At the moment, however, Agatha was not contemplating the male beauty being displayed about him. He was uncomfortably aware of the fact that he was surrounded by three characters who seemed increasingly unsavory. Harris, behind him, effectively cut off any escape. For all intents and purposes, Agatha was at their mercy, and somehow he did not feel that mercy was a virtue with which they were generously endowed.

"As I understand it," Anna addressed him, her voice so low it was almost a purr, "You offered to pay a reward to get your pup back, am I correct?"

"Yes," Agatha agreed. "Fifty dollars." He pulled his billfold hastily from his pocket, eager to pay the ransom, which was how he now regarded it, and make his escape. The matter of payment, however, was not to be left up to him. No sooner was the billfold in sight than Harris had reached around him and deftly, but firmly taken it from his hand. Agatha stood in shocked silence as Harris tossed it to Anna, who remained on the sofa in her reclining position.

She flicked it open and quite nonchalantly removed all of the money. It was not a great amount, although Agatha was well aware that there was more than fifty dollars. Anna frowned, removed a five-dollar bill from the bundle, and returned that to his billfold. The rest she stuffed inside the bra of her outfit before tossing the billfold back toward Agatha. He dropped it, and shook as he stooped to retrieve it.

"That all you have with you?" she asked coldly.

Agatha remembered his checkbook, in the breast pocket of his jacket. Instinctively, his hand went toward it. He caught himself, but not before the gesture had been observed. With a grin, the one in the posing strap stepped toward him and neatly removed the checkbook, tossing that also to Anna. She opened it and studied the figures.

"Write a check for all but ten dollars," she instructed, holding the checkbook out to Agatha.

Agatha hesitated, but there was a flicker of movement from the hand that held the cat-o'-nine-tails. He had no choice but to comply with her instructions. With a shaking hand he made out a check for ninety-five dollars, at the same time silently thanking himself for always keeping the bulk of his money in savings accounts.

"Whom shall I make this to?" he asked.

"Leave that part blank," she instructed him. "I'll take care of that."

He tore, out the check and handed that to her, pocketing the checkbook. There was little left they could ask for, unless it was his watch. Fortunately, he had not taken time to put on any other jewelry. He thought of his collection of rings: diamonds, rubies, even a genuine emerald. Undoubtedly he would have lost them.

"Is that all?" he asked, barely able to keep his voice under control.

The three of them exchanged glances. The one in the posing strap, who stood framed in the doorway, leaning against the woodwork, hooked a thumb slowly and meaningfully in the top of the posing strap, and pulled it slowly down, stretching the flimsy material, until the view was almost total.

Agatha swallowed, unable to remove his eyes from the sight. They were toying with him, he knew, and obviously this one was enjoying the game, because the flesh inside the pouch was growing larger.

Agatha thought of their cruel, merciless minds, and he remembered the instruments of torture about the room, the abundance of leather, rope, and chains. He suddenly realized that to accept the bait, he would be committing himself to their desires, and he was sure those desire would not be as pleasant as the prize now being offered to him.

He glanced about. Harris had opened the front

of his jeans, to reveal just a glimpse, but a highly tempting one, of what he had to offer.

"No thanks," Agatha managed to stammer, forcing his gaze away from the enticing flesh.

"Why not?" Anna persisted. "You like guys. There are two pretty gorgeous ones here. Take your pick. Which one do you want? Or both? Or maybe all three of us?"

Harris chuckled at that, which only caused Agatha to redden with embarrassment. His mind worked swiftly. "I can't," he insisted. "You see, well, I'm having some trouble."

"What kind of trouble?" Anna's voice turned icy, and her smile faded.

"I started burning last night, and…." his stammering was not pretended. "Well, I think I've caught something."

They were obviously disappointed, but just as obviously no, longer interested in any fun and games with him.

Anna gave a nod toward the hallway. "Okay, beat it, and take your pup."

Agatha was only too happy to comply. He half expected them to change their minds, but to his relief Harris stepped well out of his way. Apparently the fear of contamination was more than his lust. Agatha fairly flew down the hall, afraid to pause or to look back. As he emerged from the front door, he heard the three of them break into raucous laughter, but he was too eager to get away to care how much amusement they derived from him.

With Cynthia in his arms, he nearly ran to his car. Not until he was in it, and driving away, did he allow himself to breathe with relief.

When he had put several blocks between himself and the house, he pulled to the curb. His hands were shaking violently, and his heart still threatened to burst out of his chest. He sat, breathing deeply, trying to calm himself.

One thing was evident: the story of finding Cynthia on the streets had been a lie. He had been in the midst of the dognappers themselves. And judging from the number of dogs in their kitchen, it was apparent that this was no chance theft on their part, but only a art of a large-scale operation.

Anger replaced Agatha's nervousness as he again started the car up. He had learned a lesson, an expensive one. But the three he had just left were due for a lesson as well, and unless, he was mistaken, Agatha thought he knew just who could teach them that lesson.

♠ CHAPTER THREE ♠
λ

Jackie paused at the entrance to the building and checked the names at the mailboxes. He found the name he was looking for: F. Fan, Apartment C. Beneath this someone had penciled in "upstairs."

It was not a very fashionable building. The stairs creaked ominously as he climbed, careful of his step in the dim light.

Apartment C was the first one at the top. Jackie knocked loudly, ignoring the damp, mildewed odor of the building.

The knock was answered quickly, as though the occupant of that dingy little apartment had been waiting for someone, anyone, to knock at the door. Jackie's only regret was that it was not the opportunity for which she had probably been waiting.

High Camp's files on Fury Fan had been reasonably complete, even including a photograph taken when she had been at her peak as a stripper, playing in better burlesque houses throughout the country. Unfortunately, that had been quite a few years before—before she had grown too old and worn out to play as a stripper, except in some pretty shabby houses—before she had turned to hustling to try to make an occasional buck.

He wondered, as he saw the woman in the doorway, what an ex-stripper did to make a buck when she was even too old and worn out for hustling. There weren't any pensions in her field, nothing to look forward to but gruesome tenement apartments.

Her hair was still more or less blonde, although the dye job had been a bad one, leaving it streaked and uneven. And combing was apparently a luxury she rarely resorted to any more. She still made up her face, but the mascara and shadow only made her tired, hollow eyes seem the more tragic, nor lid the lipstick, badly smeared across her mouth, add the color she had presumably hoped for. She slumped, and the cheap kimono she wore did nothing to hide a body grown flabby and shapeless. It was hard to imagine that this grotesque old woman was Fury Fan herself, once billed as the Goddess of Sex.

"Miss Fan?" he greeted her, hoping without hope that he might be mistaken in his identification.

"That's me," she admitted with a listless smile. "Look, if it's about the TV payments…."

Jackie smiled and shook his head. "No money. I'm just a friend. My name is Jackie Holmes, and I'd like to talk to you about something, if I may."

She looked him up and down, briefly and bluntly. "Sure," she said finally, stepping back to permit him entrance to the one room apartment. "Come on in. I've got plenty of time."

There was another woman in the room, seated at a card table. He had apparently interrupted a game of gin. This one, a redhead in no better state of repair than Fury, studied him with frank but not unfriendly curiosity.

"My roommate," Fury introduced her companion. "O. K. Howls. Maybe you've heard of her as O. K. Plenty? We used to play together in the houses. O. K. played the Palace once, on the same bill with Harry Lauder."

"I've heard about that show," Jackie lied. "I always wondered where you went after that."

O. K. grinned, revealing more blank spaces than teeth. "What a line, huh, Fury? I was out of the business before this kid was out of diapers." She was pleased though, and Jackie was glad he had flattered her.

"What can we do for you" Fury asked, a little more friendly herself.

"I'd like to talk to you. I understand a few months ago you had a dog stolen."

The friendly atmosphere vanished in a twinkling. O. K.'s painted lips closed over the blank spaces, and Fury instinctively pulled her kimono closed.

"What are you, a cop?" she asked coldly.

"Officially, no." Jackie had decided to be as honest with them as possible. "I work for a private organization, one I'm sure you've never heard of. We've heard about some dognapping, and frankly we didn't like what we heard. My job is to try to get to the bottom of it. But to do that, I need information."

They studied him coldly for a moment. It was Fury who finally relented. "Oh, what the hell, okay."

"Huh?" her companion responded.

"Don't be stupid, I just said…forget it. What do you need to know, kid?"

"Just what happened," Jackie said. "Tell me about the dog, and about the theft, and anything you know about the people who stole him."

"Not much to tell." Fury picked up a can of beer from the table and took a healthy swig. "Cute little pooch. If you want to know, we both loved that mutt."

"What kind of dog was it?" Jackie asked.

"A poodle, and a damn good one, too, you could see that just looking at him. Furthermore, he was a gift from a John."

"That's a trick," O. K. explained, eager to share in the limelight.

"Not much of a trick, I'll admit." Fury took over the narrative again. "He was a young guy; had hot pants. We were nice to him. Hell, we knew he didn't have any money, but he was a cute little thing, hung like wow, and nice. We used to let him stop by a few times a week, just so we could get a look at that pretty young boy. Well, anyway he moved away. I think Mama heard about us and wanted to get him some place safe. But, see, before he left, he brought us the dog, as a gift. Said it was worth some money, and that would repay us for, well, for being nice. Like all we needed was another mouth to feed."

"Come off it," O. K. interrupted again. "You loved that mutt, like he was your own son."

Fury laughed, but it was a bitter laugh. "She's calling me a bitch, I guess. Yeah, I loved the dog. We both did. Cute as a button, even when it peed on my good slippers. They was satin, specially dyed red to match a dress I own."

"How did the dog—what was his name?"

"Just Dog, that's all. Sometimes we called him Mutt."

"How did he get stolen?"

Fury tried the beer can again, found it empty, and took a swig from O. K.'s instead, which earned her a dirty look.

"I took him to the store down the street one day. Tied him outside. I didn't think anybody'd be cheap enough to steal a dog, but some son-of-a-bitch did. I came out and the dog was gone."

"I cried like a baby," O. K. said, as though she might do so again without much prompting.

"Did the people who stole the dog get in touch with you, for ransom or anything?" Jackie regretted the necessity of making them talk about what was obviously a painful experience. He could well imagine how much company a little dog must have been for these two aging women.

"Oh, sure." Fury's voice had gone bitter again. "I even advertised, put a notice up at the supermarket, you know, that sort of thing. Talked to kids around the neighborhood. Well, I got a call from some guy, said he'd found the dog. I was really tickled, I'll tell you. We wanted the pooch back."

"Did he ask for money?"

"Yeah, wanted to know was there a reward. So I said sure, I'd give him ten bucks to bring the dog back. Do you know, he said make it fifty. Hell, I didn't have fifty bucks. To be honest, we didn't even have ten between us, but I figured when he got here with the dog, we could talk him into a deal."

"Did he agree?"

Fury snorted angrily and proceeded to finish off O. K.'s beer. "The bastard said fifty or nothing. So I got mad and told him to screw himself. I hung up on him, but I figured he'd call back in a little bit and say okay."

Jackie waited for her to continue. When the pause became a lengthy one, he prodded her on in a gentle tone. "What happened?"

"Couple days later, we got a box delivered to us." Her voice nearly broke as she said the words, so softly that Jackie had to strain to hear them.

His skin crawled as the implication hit home. "The dog?" he asked, hating the necessity of asking.

"They killed it," O. K. answered for her friend. "Can you figure that out, killed a poor little mutt, and then sent it back to us in a box. What kind of sicko would do a thing like that, I ask you?"

Jackie felt his temper flaring. It was as cruel an act as he had ever encountered, the act of a warped mind. In that moment, he vowed that he would leave no stone unturned until he found the person, or persons, responsible for such a beastly crime.

Fury wiped the back of a hand across her nose, and sniffed loudly. "Well, that's it."

"Did you report it to the police?"

Both of them grunted loudly, and he remembered that they had no reason to be fond of policemen.

"If it's any consolation," he said, realizing that his interview was over. "I've made myself a promise to find these people. It won't bring your dog back, but I can assure you, I'll see that these fiends pay for their acts."

Fury gave him a grateful smile. "You know, I think you mean it too."

For a moment, the ghost of her former beauty hovered about her. He saw it in her eyes, in the toss of her head as she straightens herself up. "You're a nice kid," she said in a softened voice. "You in a hurry, or you want to stay around for a while?"

Jackie gave her a warm smile, and reached for his billfold, slipping out a ten dollar bill. "I can't today," he answered, handing her the bill. "But I'll pay in advance, and collect the next time, all right?"

She held the bill lightly, fondling it between her first finger and thumb as though she hadn't seen one in a long time. Then, with a wistful sigh, she handed it back.

"Huh uh, no tickee, no laundry. I built a repu-tation on satisfied customers. When you get it, and like it, then you pay. Besides, I kind of got a notion that's not your cup of tea."

He smiled and returned the money to his bill-fold. "I'll let you know when I find them," he prom-ised.

"Do that," O. K. answered. "I'd like to give that bastard a punch in the nose, just for the hell of it."

Jackie paused on his way out. "Thanks for your help," he said to both of them. "By the way, there is one thing I would like. Maybe next time the two of you will do your routines for me. I heard they were great."

They both giggled and beamed like schoolgirls. It was Fury, however, who regained her composure first. "I'll warn you right now, we don't give free shows. You want first class entertainment, you gotta pay for it."

Jackie nodded, his face sober. "I know, but good entertainment is so hard to find these days, it would be worth paying a nice price to see some for a change.

With that, he left, leaving behind him two pleased and smiling ladies.

* * * * * * *

Three small boys had stopped to admire Jackie's car where it was parked at the street. He gave them a friendly grin as he passed them and climbed inside, flicking on the powerful engine. He was accustomed to the fact that the car attracted stares. It had been his own design, and built specially to his specifications. The Campmobile Rich jokingly designated it, and in fact it was built with his work for C.A.M.P. in mind.

Long, low, and jet black, the car exuded an aura of power, nor was the impression false. Beneath the long hood a five hundred horsepower engine waited to propel the car along the highway at breakneck speed—speed was sometimes the deciding factor in Jackie's work. Every convenience, too, had been provided: not only air conditioning, automatic window and seat adjustments, individually sculptured seats, stereophonic music, but an array of instruments and accessories of Jackie's own invention.

A cigarette dispenser handed the already lit cigarette to the driver in platinum fingers. At the push of a button, fresh coffee was dispensed into a special tray, gyroscopically kept level so that it could not spill despite the car's motion. A switch turned on a tape recorder, and even as the voice was being recorded, the notes were being typed electronically. A miniature cooking unit could prepare a meal for him in three minutes.

If necessary, the interior could be converted into sleeping accommodations, complete with bath and vanity facilities. A bevy of controls permitted him to take photos from any angle inside or outside the car, photos which were developed and printed for him within seconds.

Radio and television gave him worldwide communication capabilities, and the car had been engineered for safety. Collision was impossible, thanks to a cushion of air that could be projected completely around the car, totally absorbing any impact. From his place behind the wheel, Jackie could operate any number of weapons: battering rams, guns, tear gas cannons, listening and tracking devices. An arsenal and crime laboratory on wheels was not a luxury in Jackie's case, but a valuable tool in his fight against crime.

The silence of the car was interrupted suddenly by the sound of music. It was an old song, one rarely heard in the present, but the strains of "Lavender Blue" meant more to Jackie than nostalgia: it was a signal from Rich. Jackie threw the switch that put him in immediate contact with Rich.

"What's up?" he asked.

"A call from Lady Agatha," Rich explained. "He's got news on the dognapping, wants to see you right away."

"I'm on my way." Jackie took the corner before him with total ease, despite his high speed, and headed in the direction of Agatha's apartment. After his visit with Fury Fan and O. K. Howls, he was more than eager for a lead on the dognappers.

* * * * * * *

Agatha greeted him with relief and excitement. "Thank Heaven you're here," he exclaimed. "I got Cynthia back, and I met the dognappers."

"You met them?" Jackie paused to give Cynthia a brief pat in the way of greeting. "You mean they've been here?"

"No, I was there, at their place."

"That's even better. Tell me the details, everything you can remember."

He listened in silence as Agatha explained about all that had happened, beginning with the call from Mark Harris. His expression turned grim when he heard that Agatha had gone alone to the house.

"That was foolish," he pointed out. "You might have walked into a hornet's nest."

"As it turned out, I did, but I just wasn't thinking. I was so excited by the possibility of getting Cynthia back." He continued the story. As he listened, Jackie grew increasingly angry. His guess had been right: they were dealing with an organized ring, and a ruthless bunch they were, too.

"You were lucky to get out with your skin intact," he said when Agatha had concluded. "That was quick thinking on your part to make them believe you had an infection. Otherwise, I shudder to think what indecencies they might have inflicted on you."

"I got the impression they weren't, oh, I can't quite put my finger on it. I guess they just didn't seem normal in some way."

"They aren't," Jackie assured him. "From what I've learned, their minds are warped." Briefly, he told of his visit to Fury Fan's apartment.

"How terrible," Agatha exclaimed when he heard the climax of the story. "And to think that might have happened to my little Cynthia."

The doorbell rang, bringing Agatha to his feet. "Can't imagine who that would be," he said, hurrying toward the door.

They were both surprised to see Don, the young redhead they had met at the Westgate the evening of Cynthia's theft.

"I know I should have called," he said. "But I found myself in the neighborhood, and thought I'd call to see if anything has happened regarding your dog."

"That is a coincidence," Agatha answered. "I just got her back today, but come on in. You remember Jackie, don't you?"

It seemed to Jackie that Don was a little embarrassed at finding him there. Jackie found himself wondering if he had been mistaken about Don's attraction for him. Perhaps after all it had been Agatha in whom Don was interested.

"Nice seeing you again," Jackie nevertheless greeted him cordially.

"Same here," Don said, "But tell me about the dog. How on earth did you get her back?"

Agatha went through his story again, this time with more relish. Now that the danger was past, and his nerves were calmed, he was obviously beginning to enjoy the excitement of his adventure.

"It was quite an experience," he concluded. "But at least I did get Cynthia back, and this theft may bring about the capture of the dognappers."

"Oh, really, how is that?" Don asked, openly interested.

Jackie sensed that Agatha was on the verge of divulging too much, particularly about C.A.M.P. Jackie headed off the conversation abruptly.

"He means that they've revealed their identities, and their whereabouts. I think, Agatha, the first thing for you to do is to notify the police."

"Yes, I suppose I should have done that right away," Agatha agreed, catching the warning glance Jackie threw in his direction. He moved toward the phone.

"Isn't that a little foolish?" Don suggested.

Both of them stared at him, puzzled. "Why foolish?" Jackie asked. "This is a police matter, after all, they were notified of the theft. They should be informed of all these details."

Don shrugged, and lit a cigarette. "I suppose you're probably right. But personally, I don't see that it can accomplish anything. You have no evidence, for one thing, except your word against theirs, and there were three of them. It's not like kidnapping people, remember? The dogs can't provide any evidence."

"It's possible the police couldn't make a case stick, not yet at least," Jackie agreed. "But if nothing else, it will throw a scare into the gang."

"Maybe. On the other hand, they obviously have Agatha's name, address, even telephone number. What happens if they decide to retaliate?"

"I hadn't thought of that," Agatha agreed somberly. Obviously it was not a pleasant thought.

"Even if you stopped payment on the check, there's nothing to prevent them from coming here and doing some real damage."

He paused in his argument. "I wonder if I can use your bathroom for a moment?" he asked.

"Certainly, it's straight through there," Agatha pointed the way absentmindedly.

When he was gone, Agatha turned anxiously to Jackie. "Jackie, he's right. If I go to the police, there's little they can do. And those criminals are just beastly enough to want to get back at me."

"Even so, I think it should be reported. Criminals such as these depend upon the fear of their victims. When people give in to them, it only makes them stronger."

"I know all that, but couldn't you look into it for me? If C.A.M.P. went after them, they might not suspect me of being behind it. And at least I'd feel safer."

Jackie considered the matter for a moment. He still felt that the police should be kept informed of the situation, in all its details. Nonetheless, he did not really have the right to insist that Agatha endanger himself, and in that respect, Don had been right:

these criminals were vicious enough, and warped enough, to retaliate in some way.

"Very well," he agreed reluctantly. "I'll go to this place, and see what I can accomplish. But you must understand that C.A.M.P. is not in a position to work outside the law."

"But you're so wonderful, I know you'll find a way of proving them guilty. I'll write down the instructions for getting there. No, wait, I still have the slip that I wrote them on." He found the note, and handed it to Jackie. Jackie slipped the note into his pocket as Don reentered the room.

"I'll be on my way, then," Jackie said, standing. "I'll call you, Agatha, if I hear any news."

"We've decided you were right," Agatha informed Don.

"I think that's wise," Don stated. He turned to Jackie. "I don't suppose you could give me a lift? I didn't bring my car today."

"Sure," Jackie agreed readily. He was still more than a little attracted to the shapely redhead. It was Agatha's turn to be disappointed.

"I thought maybe you'd want to stay for a drink," he offered hopefully to Don.

"Next time, I promise. I've got some things I have to attend to this afternoon."

Jackie led the way to his car. Don was impressed by the vehicle. "What kind of car is this?" he asked, slipping into the passenger's seat.

"I had it especially made," Jackie admitted.

"You must be quite wealthy."

"I am," Jackie said simply, starting the car with a roar. They moved swiftly away from the curb. "Which way do I go?"

Don gave him instructions as they traveled. Fortunately, the address was not out of the way for Jackie. A few minutes later, he pulled up in front of an ordinary-looking apartment building.

"Aren't you coming up?" Don asked when Jackie made no move to switch off the engine. "I've been sort of hoping we could get together."

"I'd love to," Jackie said sincerely. "But I can't just now. I have to get back and feed my dog."

"You have one too? It sounds like I'm the only one without an animal to feed. What kind is yours?"

"A poodle. And a very unique one, I might add."

"Unique? In what way?"

Jackie grinned. "It would take too long to tell you all about her. Anyway, if you're curious, maybe I can coax you over to see me some day."

"I'm free tonight, if you want to come by later," Don offered.

Jackie allowed himself a quick glance in the direction of his companion's lap. Don was still a very tempting morsel, and with any kind of luck, he would still have part of the evening free.

"I can probably come by about nine," he agreed. "If you're going to be here."

"I'll be here," Don assured him with a pleased grin.

Jackie waited until the young man had disappeared into the apartment building. The temptation to linger for a few minutes, and go in with the handsome redhead, had been very strong, but business came first, and right now he had some business with a group of dognappers.

He started off again, in the direction of the house where Agatha had met the dognappers. At the moment, he did not know just what he was going to do when he got there. He could scarcely barge in and give them all what they deserved, but he was confident, as he drove, that something would present itself to him. He had dealt with such people before, under devilish circumstances. There had been times, too, when he had seemed doomed to defeat. One thing, however, gave him the courage and the inspiration that served him so well in his never-ending war against crime and injustice.

Ultimately, he knew that right would prevail.

♠ CHAPTER FOUR ♠
λ

Jackie found the house without any difficulty, exactly as Agatha had described it to him. He drove past it and parked a short distance away. At the moment there was no sign of life about the place. He left the car and made his way toward the house, his senses alert.

The ringing of the doorbell echoed inside the house. Jackie waited for a long moment, listening for a movement inside. He was about to ring again when the door opened slightly. Through the thin opening, Jackie could see an almost unbroken expanse of bare flesh. It appeared that the man behind the door was totally nude, but Jackie recalled Agatha's description, and decided that this was the one in the posing strap. Maybe, he thought with concealed amusement, it was all the fellow had to wear.

"Yes?" the stranger asked suspiciously.

"Mr. Harris?"

"He ain't here," was the reply. "What do you want?"

Jackie shifted his weight from one foot to the other, trying to create an impression of nervous helplessness. "I've lost a dog, one that I'm very fond of. Someone told me that Mr. Harris might be able to help me find her."

"Who told you that?" The door inched slightly closed.

Jackie shrugged. "I don't know, a stranger in a bar. He said he understood Harris had found a dog recently. I should explain, it's rather a valuable dog. I'll pay highly to get her back."

"Yeah?" That comment produced the desired results. The door moved slightly open again, and there was a new interest in the voice. Jackie had guessed that the man was alone in the house, and it was his hope that the offer would sound to him like an unexpected landfall, a chance to pick up some extra cash and score a surprise bonus for his companions.

"Of course, if you don't have a dog here...." Jackie said wistfully, stepping back from the door as his voice trailed off. He had already heard the sniffing and whining from inside, and he was fully aware that there were numerous dogs inside the house.

"Wait a minute." The stranger stepped back from the door, opening it wider. "Come on in."

"Then you do have a stray dog?" Jackie asked eagerly, stepping inside without hesitation. The door was closed quickly behind him. He was inside the house, with at least one of the dognappers.

Agatha had not exaggerated in describing the physical beauty of the young men involved. This one was as beautiful as he was dangerous looking: an almost cruelly handsome face, with a magnificently sculpted body, naked to view except for the posing strap he still wore. And he was certainly aware that his body was being admired.

"Are you Mr. Harris?" Jackie asked, not bothering to conceal his admiration for the stranger's beauty.

"No, I'm Jay. Jay Cleland."

"My name is Percy," Jackie answered. "Percy Wilde." He glanced around, in the direction of the kitchen door. He could see the bevy of dogs, just as Agatha had described. "Heavens, you do have a number of pets, don't you? Is my Marmaduke here? She's a dachshund."

"There is a dachshund." Jay stepped to the door and pointed across the room. "There, in the corner. Is that yours?"

Jackie stared for a moment, then shook his head sadly. "No, I'm afraid not," he said. "What a disappointment."

"Yeah, that is too bad." Plainly Jay was dis-appointed that he might not be able to get the money he had hoped for.

Jackie moved slightly for the door. "Well, I'm sure you must be very busy, Mr. Cleland, and I've caused you so much bother already. I suppose I may as well be on my way."

"I'm not busy," Jay informed him. "I got plenty of time to kill." He had decided apparently on the next best approach for making some money out of his visitor.

Jackie allowed himself to pause, interest showing on his face. "Well, I'm not really in a hurry," he said.

Jay was posing provocatively, and smiling now that his hint had been picked up. "You must have a lot of money," he said.

"Some," Jackie agreed. His eyes roamed up and down Jay's lovely body. "My, you do have a gorgeous physique."

Jay preened like a peacock. "Nice, ain't it? Lot's of guys have tried to make it with me."

Jackie ran his tongue over his lips. "Do you, ummm, do that sort of thing?"

"Sometimes. Depends on how nice they are to me."

Jackie paused thoughtfully for a moment. "You mean you want money?" he asked. When Jay nodded, he added, "That's understandable. A body like yours should be of some value."

Jay was becoming more and more interested. His narrow eyes gleamed. "It is," he agreed. He dropped a hand to the posing strap and rubbed. His body was quickly responsive; the thin fabric tautened and stretched as the flesh within hardened and began to rise. Nor did the filmy material leave anything to the imagination. The pink flesh was plainly visible through the fabric.

Jackie did not have to pretend his admiration, or his desire. Evil or not, Jay was an enticing specimen.

"How much is it usually worth?" he asked.

Jay shrugged. "How much you got on you?"

Jackie thought for a moment. "Close to a hundred dollars," he replied.

Jay was beaming by this time, and the prospect of that much money only added to his sexual responses. Jackie wondered how long the flimsy material over his now blatantly revealed flesh would endure being stretched to such limits. As a matter of fact, he was wondering how long he would endure being stretched to such limits.

"That should be enough," Jay announced. "There's a bedroom back here."

Jay led the way through the house. They passed through the den that Agatha had described, into the large bedroom. There was only one bed, nearly twice the size of a king-size. Apparently, Jackie found himself thinking, they all slept together. But then, from Agatha's descriptions, he had suspected they were a perverted lot. He undressed, unobtrusively sizing up the room. There was only one door out of it, back through the den. If anything went wrong, he might be trapped here. His eyes moved about, noticing the windows. One of them was open, and it was only a one-story house. In a pinch, that would serve him as an exit.

Almost unnecessarily, Jay had removed the posing strap. Jackie had no trouble becoming aroused by the Greek God before him. He felt a pang of regret that such a beautiful creature should have become so warped in his mind. It was such a loss to decent society.

As he moved toward the bed, Jackie decided that, in Jay's case, instruments of torture were superfluous. He already had a built-in instrument that could undoubtedly inflict as much pain, or more, than any of the devices on display in the den. How, he wondered, had anyone ever managed to accommodate this creature? For that matter, just how was he going to manage it? The answer came to him in a flash. He knew all at once how he could derive some pleasure from this escapade, and at the same time repay in a small measure some of the pain that Jay had caused others.

They embraced, fondling one another experimentally. Jay was not, Jackie decided, a very inspired lover. Mostly he just wanted to be admired and fawned over. For a moment Jackie did just that, reaching down to stroke the blazing rock-hard flesh being offered him. It was tempting to try it, but he had other plans.

"Think you can take it?" Jay asked with a smirk. Jackie had no doubt that the man derived his greatest pleasure from knowing he was subjecting his companions to great agonies.

"To be honest," Jackie replied, "I was planning on trying it." He added to the comment by slipping his hand meaningfully under Jay's firm buttocks, reaching for the warm valley between the twin hills.

It was a moment before Jay understood. When he did, he stiffened slightly, growing tense. "Don't get any ideas about that," he said firmly. "I don't go that route."

"Oh?" Jackie sat up slightly. "But I thought you understood, that's what I was willing to pay so highly for."

"Oh, no," Jay snapped, taking himself in his hand. "You're paying for this."

Jackie glanced downward with a lack of interest. "I see. Well, it's very splendid, of course, but my interests don't lie there." He got up from the bed and reached for his trousers.

He had counted on Jay's greed coming to the fore, and it did. The man didn't want to lose the money that had been offered. "Look," he said quickly, "How about a deal? We make it my way, for half the amount, okay?"

"No thanks," Jackie replied. He began dressing—slowly, however, for he was convinced he would win.

Jay fidgeted uncomfortably. "Gee, like I told you, I just can't. I never let anyone do that to me before."

"It's all right," Jackie assured him. "I'm not angry. I understand that money isn't that important to you."

For a moment Jay was silent. "Will it hurt much?" he asked finally in a hesitant tone.

"Not unless you're a real baby," Jackie answered, pausing in the act of fastening his belt.

Jay frowned unhappily, but he yielded. With a curt "Okay," he turned over on his stomach on the bed.

Jackie undressed much faster than he had dressed. In a minute, he was back on the bed, kneeling over the prostrate form. He smiled as he advanced toward his goal.

"Ain't you going to use anything?" Jay asked, turning his head to look back over his shoulder.

"I'll be careful," Jackie assured him without pausing. His flesh met flesh. Slowly but firmly he pushed forward. For a long moment the inexperienced flesh resisted the advance. Then it began gradually to yield. Jay groaned.

"I thought it wouldn't hurt," he protested. "It's killing me already."

GOOD, Jackie wanted to say, but didn't. Instead he said, "Just relax, and think about the money. It'll be better in a minute."

The mention of the money performed its expected magic. It was obvious that the experience was an agony for the young man beneath him, but Jay's protests limited themselves to smothered groans as Jackie pushed viciously forward. At last an entrance was gained, the warm flesh embracing Jackie tightly.

Jackie paused from the effort, and it was a considerable effort. One thing was certain, Jay had not lied in saying this was the first time. *By the time I'm finished with you,* Jackie thought, *It'll be the last, too.*

He arched his back, and thrust forward again, not gently, as he would ordinarily have done with an inexperienced partner, but hard and deep, deliberately being as cruel as possible. This time the smothered groan was an actual yelp. Unrelenting, Jackie thrust again, still deeper, tearing his way into the virgin passage. He thrust again, completely losing himself within the trembling body. He was not as large as Jay himself, but he knew full well he was far from small. This would have been a painful experience for someone well versed in this art. He knew it was sheer torture for the burly Jay.

He withdrew, until the union was almost nonexistent; then, in a violent lunge, he again entered completely, literally knocking the wind from his companion. Again and again he withdrew and lunged, in a vicious fury. Jay could no longer contain his agony. He was yelling and squirming, scarcely able to endure.

"Stop," he cried aloud, "I can't stand it, not even for the money."

"It's almost over," Jackie hissed in his ear, using all of his strength to keep the body pinned beneath his. Jay was struggling in earnest now to escape the onslaught, but Jackie had been truthful in saying it was almost over. As though riding a bucking bronc, Jackie held to the kicking, struggling body beneath him, lunging savagely. His climax was rushing to him at breakneck speed, sweeping over him. With a cry of satisfaction, he exploded within the twisting body.

The room exploded at the same time. It seemed as though the top had blown off Jackie's head. A million lights blazed brilliantly, an unbelievable cascade of fireworks erupted. It lasted for an instant only, too briefly for him to realize what had happened. Then, mercifully, he plunged into unconsciousness.

THE MAN FROM C.A.M.P.

♠ CHAPTER FIVE ♠
λ

Consciousness returned slowly. It seemed an eternity that Jackie had been spinning through black oblivion; then, gradually, the spinning slowed.

Suddenly he remembered: Jay, the bed, a pounding sex scene, climax—then, someone had hit him from behind, knocking him out.

His eyes flew open as he sat up. The movement sent a fresh shock wave of pain through his head, but he ignored that. It was dark, and he was certainly not in the bed with Jay. He stumbled to his feet, staring around him at grass and trees.

Recognition dawned on him finally. He was in Griffith Park. Apparently Jay and the accomplice who had come upon the scene had brought him here and dumped him in one of the more secluded areas. His watch told him it was after eight o'clock, which meant he had been here nearly an hour.

He groaned faintly as he remembered that his car was still there, near Jay's house. He looked around again to get his bearings, and began walking in the direction that would take him out of the park.

He was not far from the road, but it was still a long walk to get out of the vast park. And time was important. He had a score now to settle with his friends in the house in Silverlake, and every moment that he was gone gave them an advantage.

He reached the street at last, and turned in the direction of Silverlake. Luck was with him; a taxi passed by a few minutes later. He waved it down, and he was on his way back to Silverlake. Luckily, although his assailants had taken the wallet from his pocket they had not found the stash that he kept hidden in his shoe.

His car was still where he had left it, apparently untouched. Fortunately, even had it been recognized as his, it was safe. The doors were opened only by concealed mechanisms that would be very difficult to discover. Jackie paid off the cab driver, and opened his car.

At his touch a concealed compartment slid from beneath the dash. He opened it, and removed the gun hidden there, a tiny, jeweled Derringer. Like him, it appeared to be little more than a harmless toy, but in the right circumstances, it could be deadly. It was an item he carried for use only as a last resort, but he knew from experience that the sight of a gun was usually sufficient, without the necessity of firing it.

The house was dark as he approached it. Jackie hesitated as he drew near, then passed the house. A short distance beyond it was an alley. He took this, making his way toward the rear. When he was past the house, he stopped in the tall shadows of the shrubbery that surrounded the house. There were no lights on inside, or any signs of life.

It was possible that his "friends" had made an escape, but it was also possible that they were still inside the house, confident that they had frightened him sufficiently to discourage any further interest on his part. He reminded himself that they had no way of knowing he was anyone other than Percy Wilde, the name he had given Jay upon his arrival. Yet that fact struck him as puzzling. If they had no reason to suspect his true identity, why had he been struck unconscious?

Unless, of course, one of the others in the group was Jay's lover, and a jealous type. Still, from Agatha's account of his visit here, that hardly seemed to be the case.

The shrubbery ended at the back of the lot, where a low fence separated the grounds from another alley. Entering the yard was no problem. Jackie moved toward the house, careful to remain in the shadows. Still there was no movement or sound from inside the house. He studied the house and identified the window of the bedroom in which he had been with Jay. Stealthily he edged closer. The window was still open. Inside, the house was dark and silent.

He paused for a moment longer, considering the situation. If he was caught in the house, he hadn't a leg to stand on. At best, the group could have him arrested for housebreaking. Judging from what he knew of them, it was more likely they would think of something far worse. He thought of their taste for instruments of torture, but he had many times tangled with master criminals—the infamous Tiger Bey, the ruthless Big Daddy, others of their ilk. These dognappers held no fear for him.

With his senses alert, he clambered up and through the window.

The door connecting the bedroom with the den was closed. He crept toward it, pausing again, straining his ears. There was no sound. Certain of himself now, he pushed the door boldly open and stepped into the den. The silence of the house had told him they were almost certainly gone. Otherwise, he would have heard some noise from all the dogs that had been in the kitchen.

He was right in his conclusion. The den had been stripped hastily, except for the heavier furnishings. He strode quickly through the house, but the rest of it was equally deserted. Even the animals had been removed.

He stood in the empty kitchen, surveying the evidence of its recent occupation. There was no way the dognappers could have known his true identity but obviously they were taking no chances. Whoever had knocked him unconscious must have decided that he was a threat to their security. They had flown the coop, moving on to a new location, and his search would have to begin all over again.

He went swiftly through the house, his sharp eyes watching for any clues that might have been left behind, but there was nothing of any significance. Disappointed, he left the house by the front door and returned to his car.

It was well after nine o'clock by this time. He thought of his dog, Sophie. Fortunately, she was well accustomed to the eccentricities of his schedule, and his penthouse apartment had been designed with her needs in mind. Electronic equipment prepared and served her dinner at a preset time each evening, and she had been trained to operate a switch that opened a door onto a small roof garden, where a neat oasis of grass supplied her needs. Still, he could hardly go calling on Don in his present condition. Instead, he drove swiftly toward his apartment.

The door to his vast underground garage opened automatically at his approach. Deftly. he steered the car into one of the numerous stalls. Along the considerable length of both walls, numerous matching stalls held his large collection of automobiles, some of them, like this one, designed exclusively for him, others of classic vintage: rare Alfa Romeos, Duesenbergs, and Bentleys.

He strode quickly across the garage to the private elevator that whisked him upward to his penthouse. Jackie was a man of considerable wealth, and his manner of living reflected that wealth. In the past, he had been nothing more than a frivolous, shallow young playboy, the sole heir to a vast fortune.

It was at that time that he had developed his first real crush, on a man many years older than himself. Unknown to him, the man had become the victim of blackmailers. Bewildered, Jackie had watched as his idol unaccountably went downhill, until finally he had committed suicide.

When the truth had been revealed, Jackie had vowed that he would somehow find a way to save others from that same tragedy. Fate had stepped into the picture then, in the form of two men from the then fledgling organization, C.A.M.P. They had known, in some mysterious way, of Jackie's affection for his idol, and of the tragedy that had occurred. It had not been difficult to persuade the young multi-millionaire to join the organization, and train for a future of crime fighting.

His poodle, Sophie, rushed to greet him at the door. Seeing her as she was now, yipping, jumping, tail wagging furiously, one would have suspected her to be the epitome of harmlessness. In fact, like Jackie, she had been rigorously trained to serve the needs of C.A.M.P. The teeth, that seemed so harmless, were kept at razor sharpness. A single command from Jackie could turn her into a wild beast, a killer who knew neither fear nor mercy. Her fine training, vicious teeth, keen reflexes, her incredible senses of smell and hearing, all combined to make her a formidable enemy of any wrongdoers.

At the moment, however, she was merely a happy puppy, delighted to see her master. Jackie took a few minutes to play with her. Often it was necessary to neglect her literally for days, but in her own way she seemed to understand, and she was content with these brief times when his attention was solely hers.

Finally, carrying her in his arms, Jackie hurried to the phone and placed a call to Don. He was flattered to notice that the phone was answered after the first ring. The attractive young man must have been sitting practically on top of it.

"I got tied up," Jackie apologized. "And I'm just now getting back to my apartment. If you don't mind my being a little late, I could be there within an hour."

"I'll be waiting," Don assured him.

When he had finished the call, Jackie placed another one to his friend, Vernon Boswell. Boswell was owner of one of the cities leading newspapers, as well as a long time personal friend. Likewise, Boswell knew of C.A.M.P. and Jackie's association with the organization. On more than one occasion he had proved of invaluable assistance in solving a case. For this reason, the number that Jackie dialed was not the one that would be used by any other of Boswell's associates. Jackie alone knew that this number, and its use was a certain signal to Boswell that his aid was needed urgently.

The phone rang once, which was followed by a clicking and buzzing combination. The sound told Jackie that Boswell was not at his home, and that the automatic control on his phone was transferring the call to whichever location he was in. When the call was answered, Jackie guessed from background noises that Boswell was in his car, probably on one of the city's freeways.

"What's up, Jackie?" Boswell's gruff voice answered.

"I need some help," Jackie explained, not bothering with niceties of conversation. They were both men of action, and they had long since agreed that such conventions were not essential in their friendship. "Can you get a story into tomorrow's paper for me, a rather large spread?"

"It's late, but it can be done," Boswell agreed. "Give me the details."

"I need a spread on Sophie," Jackie said. "You have pictures of the two of us, and plenty of trivia in your files. Treat her as a unique and priceless animal. And be certain to mention my name and pinpoint the location of my apartment."

"Can do," Boswell assured him. "Will there be a story in it for us when you're finished?"

"I hope so," Jackie said. "And I'll see that you get the scoop."

"Fine. Don't worry, by tomorrow morning, Sophie will be a celebrity."

With that business completed, Jackie busied himself cleaning up and changing clothes. A short time later, he was again on his way across town, hurrying toward Don's apartment. For the moment, he had done all he could on his case. It was time now for a little pleasure.

Don answered the door promptly, smiling as he saw Jackie standing there. "Come on in," he said, opening the door wide. "The drinks are cold, and the host is hot."

"Sounds like an intriguing combination," Jackie answered, following him into the apartment. It was a single, but the studio couch had already been made into a bed. The lights were low, and the music soothing.

"Make yourself comfortable," Don suggested, indicating the inviting bed. "I'll fix us drinks. Scotch okay?"

"Fine." Jackie slipped off his shoes before reclining on the bed. He watched as Don prepared the drinks, his desire mounting as he watched the supple body move gracefully and sensuously. Unless he was mistaken, having Don would be like putting a tiger in his tank, and after his unfortunate episode with the lovely but dull Jay, he was in the mood for a little real action.

Don returned with the drinks and settled himself on the bed also, leaning cozily against Jackie. "I was beginning to think you'd never come," he said, peering through long lashes into Jackie's face.

"I'm hoping to, very soon." Jackie moved closer, kissing the warm lips hungrily. They embraced for a long moment, their mouths feeding eagerly on one another.

Jackie felt skilled hands on his clothes, carefully removing them. He offered full cooperation, lifting himself so that the trousers could be tugged off. Don was proficient at his task. In a few minutes, Jackie was naked, and his ardor quite apparent.

Don undressed also, and again they embraced. They kissed and fondled one another, occasionally stopping to sip their drinks. During one of the pauses, Don gave Jackie a mischievous grin.

"Ever had a Northern Treat?" he asked.

Jackie frowned. "Not that I know of," he said. "What is it?"

"I'll show you." Don took a long swallow from his glass, gulping two of the ice cubes into his mouth as he did so. Jackie grinned as he guessed what was coming next. It would be a new experience for him, and he loved trying anything new.

With his mouth full of ice, Don bent over him, lowering his head to Jackie's crotch. Jackie gasped as warm lips closed over his burning flesh, and again as he felt the icy touch of the ice cubes.

It was an incredible sensation, the mingling of hot and cold as Don worked on him. Jackie expected to see clouds of steam, but there were none. He could feel the ice melting, streams of chilling moisture warming as it ran over his flesh. He writhed in ecstasy.

"That's great," he gasped when Don came up for air. "Where did you ever learn that?"

"There's more, if you want to try it," Don explained. At Jackie's enthusiastic nod, he added, "I'll have to borrow your ice cubes. You melted all of mine."

Don again put the ice cubes in his mouth, swishing them around to let them melt slightly. At the same time, he opened a convenient drawer, and removed a small tube of petroleum jelly.

"Any objections?" he asked through the ice as he ran a hand across Jackie's buttocks.

"Be my guest," was Jackie's reply. He turned, arching his back to raise the lower portion of his torso in the air. The lubricant was applied carefully. Jackie waited, not quite sure what to expect.

When it came, it was a shock. He felt the numbing coldness of the cubes, their edges rounded by partial melting, penetrating into his body. Instinctively, he jerked away, but Don was prepared for that reaction, and pursued his initiative.

The painful shock was fleeting, however. In an instant, it had been replaced by chilling numbness as the frozen invader was thrust deeper. Jackie's body trembled at this new sensation, but there was still more to come. Don knelt over him, and there was another entry: larger, harder, and so hot in contrast that it seemed scorching.

"Wow!" was all Jackie could manage to say.

"Like it?" Don grunted from over his shoulder.

"It's different." Jackie could not truthfully say whether he liked the experience or not. It was like nothing he had ever imagined before, and as an

74

artist in the sexual arena, he was always interested in discovering new forms of sexual activity, and he looked upon this as an educational experience.. The searing thickness was moving deeper and deeper, and as it did so, it was forcing the numbing coldness of the ice deeper and deeper also. He could only imagine how it must feel for Don, the juxtaposition of hot and cold.

Don made it quite apparent that he was enjoying the adventure, however. His body was moving more and more rapidly, his breath loud and harsh in Jackie's ear. Jackie arched his back further, lifting himself to meet the deep, powerful thrusts.

Don cried aloud, and his body shook furiously as he reached his peak, burying himself deeply within Jackie's body. The last of the coldness vanished in the path of the searing eruption that followed. Jackie fell weakly to the surface of the bed, Don's body limp over him.

"Whew," Jackie gasped when Don finally stirred and withdrew from him. "That's quite an experience."

"You didn't mind, did you?" Don asked, concern apparent.

"Not at all," Jackie replied. "I always like to learn new tricks. To be honest, it was exciting, but I don't think I'd try it too often."

Don reached for his drink. "I'm afraid these have gotten a little warm," he said, frowning. "Want me to get some more ice?"

"Not just yet," Jackie answered, ruffling the red hair. "Right now I could use a little thawing out."

Don laughed, and glanced down at Jackie's lap. "You don't look exactly cold to me," he said. He knelt again, his tousled hair falling lightly across Jackie's bare abdomen as he moved.

Jackie watched the rising and falling of the red hair. He glanced over his companion's body, and was pleased to see that Don's excitement seemed not at all diminished. One thing was certain: his playmate was the hottest iceberg he had ever run into.

♠ CHAPTER SIX ♠
λ

It was nearly three A.M. when Jackie left the apartment. He had attempted to leave earlier, but each time Don had begged him to stay a little longer. Finally, the sexy redhead had fallen asleep, and Jackie had risen and dressed, leaving a note that he would call the next day.

The thought of home was strong in his mind as Jackie climbed into his car. The familiar strains of Lavender Blue, however, quickly dispelled that thought. It was the signal from C.A.M.P. Jackie turned on his radio.

"Yes, Rich?" he asked, at once alert and ready for any action.

"You've had a little problem," Rich replied, obviously waiting for Jackie's contact. "Someone tried to break into your apartment. The alarm sounded here, of course."

"Catch anything?"

"I sent one of the boys over, I should be hearing in a few minutes."

"I'll join you for a good night cap," Jackie said, switching off the radio. He knew without asking that the attempt had been an unsuccessful one. Without proper knowledge of the mechanisms that locked and unlocked the doors, it would be virtually impossible for anyone, to gain entrance to his penthouse. He was puzzled, however, by the attempt. Was it merely a coincidence, just another attempt at housebreaking, or was there some connection with the dognapping ring.

The fact that he owned a dog was no secret, of course. It was possible that somehow they had learned of Sophie before the appearance of the article in Boswell's newspaper, but on the other hand, there was no really likely way they could have gained that information. With that puzzle on his mind, he drove toward the C.A.M.P. offices. By this time of night, the Round Up was closed. Jackie drove to the rear, into a small parking lot. One of the many keys on his ring opened a small door that entered directly into the hall outside the restrooms. Jackie passed quickly into the office itself, where Rich was waiting to greet him.

"I heard from my man," Rich announced as he came in. "No clues left behind. The alarms frightened away whoever it was. Any idea what they were after?"

Jackie shrugged. "I've been wondering the same thing myself. They might just have been after anything they could find. Or of course, I have made a few enemies in my work over the years. It may have been someone after me. Then too, it may have been our dognapping friends, after Sophie. They concentrate on valuable animals."

"How are you doing on that case?" Rich asked, pouring drinks for both of them.

"I don't know yet," Jackie replied. He seated himself on one of the sofas, kicking off his shoes. As Rich listened attentively, Jackie explained all that had happened regarding the case, finishing with his call to Boswell, and the story that would appear in the papers the next day.

"So you're going to use Sophie as a decoy," Rich said. "It might work at that."

"I'm hoping it will," Jackie said. "Knowing Boswell, he'll make Sophie sound like the most un-usual and valuable animal since Rudolph the Red-nosed Reindeer. If these people read at all, they're bound to see the spread, and I'm sure they'll be tempted to try stealing her."

"What then?"

"I'm not sure. I'll have to play that by ear. Right now, it's up to them to make the next move."

He finished his drink and rose to go. Rich stood also.

"Things are quiet, if you want to stay for a while," Rich offered suggestively.

Jackie smiled wearily. "Not tonight. Right now I think I'm coming down with a case of frost-bite."

"Frostbite?" Rich frowned in puzzlement. "It must be close to eighty degrees outside."

"But it was a lot colder in," Jackie replied. He blew Rich a kiss as he went through the door.

At home, he took time to examine the front entrance to his apartment, which was also through a private elevator. When the elevator had failed to re-spond to the signal button, they had apparently attempted to remove the electrical plate and try working on the wires. The attempt had, of course, set off alarms, in the building and in the office of C.A.M.P.

What the intruders hadn't known, of course, was that except for Jackie's own penthouse, the building was unoccupied. Except at C.A.M.P., no one would have heard the alarms. It was well for them that they hadn't known that fact, though. Had they lingered just a few minutes longer, Rich's man would have arrived in time to apprehend them.

There was no need for him to check for fingerprints. That would have been done as a routine matter by the agent Rich had sent here, and if there were any results, Jackie would hear about them in the morning. He made his way upstairs where Sophie, aroused by the alarms, stood just outside the elevator, ready to attack any stranger who emerged. At sight of Jackie, she again became a harmless little poodle.

Jackie glanced at his watch. It was four thirty in the morning. He wanted to be up no later than eight, in readiness for any more skullduggery on the part of the dognappers. Fortunately, he had trained himself to get by on a minimum of sleep, squeezed in wherever possible in his busy schedule. By his usual standards, three hours was rather a long night's rest.

Promptly at eight the following morning, he awoke and at once began readying himself for the day. He and Sophie were just sitting down to their morning coffee when he received his first call, this one from a kennel. The gentleman on the phone, the owner of the kennel, had read the article in the morning paper, and was interested in buying Sophie.

"I'm afraid she's not for sale," Jackie replied.

"I'll pay any price, and I'm not a poor man," the voice on the phone insisted.

"Sorry," Jackie told him firmly. Boswell had apparently done a good job with the article. While he talked, Jackie pushed the button that would deliver the morning paper from the front of the building directly to the kitchen table.

The man on the phone sounded genuinely disappointed. "Well, I would like to ask one favor: may I at least see the dog?"

"Of course." Jackie made an appointment for later in the morning. When the call was completed, he radioed Rich directly and gave him the information. While Jackie waited, Rich ran the information through the files of C.A.M.P., and a moment later informed him that from all appearances the man was legitimate.

Disappointed, Jackie turned his attention to the paper that had been delivered. The spread was not hard to find. It covered most of the first two pages of the second section, complete with color photos of Sophie and Jackie in the apartment, as well as several of the many photos from Boswell's files.

The article with the photos was smoothly written, almost as though it were underplaying Sophie's many achievements. It listed briefly some of her varied awards, among them the fact that she was the only dog to have won three years running in the Westminster dog show, in three categories – best of breed, best of show, and best in obedience.

It went on to further point out that she was the only poodle ever invited to enter the National Field

Championships, as a retriever, an event in which she again took first place. And the paragraph ended with the information that she was the only dog to be awarded two honors usually reserved for humans. Her part in saving the lives of one hundred fifty children trapped in a hospital fire had earned her the Red Cross Life Saving Trophy. And a year before that, she had been awarded the Congressional Medal of Honor, the only French Poodle ever so honored, as a result of the heroism she had displayed when Jackie had loaned her briefly to the U.S. military services to assist in the rescue of some American prisoners in Viet Nam.

The article went on to describe some of her many unique accomplishments: her ability to respond to musical signals, as well as signals transmitted in Morris Code, and to read Braille with her nose, and her ability to operate much of the complex electronic equipment installed in Jackie's apartment.

Not surprisingly, the writer had concluded by describing her as Sophie, the Superdog. Jackie smiled as he remembered the name that had been attached to him on one assignment: Superfag. Well, super is as super does, the way he saw it.

"Not a bad team," he said to Sophie, who had finally decided that the coffee, with just the right amount of cream and sugar, was cooled to her taste. As she lapped at it daintily, Jackie folded the paper and carefully put it on a shelf where he was sure she would not reach it. Rich sometimes kidded him by saying he was certain Sophie could read. Jackie did not really accept that suggestion as fact, except for her rudimentary understanding of Braille, but there were times when he wasn't too certain on the sub-

82

ject. Sophie already knew that she was exceptional. It was best, he felt, not to take a chance on giving her a swelled head.

The ringing of the doorbell surprised him. As he went to answer it, he wondered if the man who had wanted to buy Sophie had come by early to try again to persuade Jackie to sell. Or maybe, he thought, walking faster, this was the response he had been hoping for, from the dognappers.

At first, he did not recognize the person on the viewing screen. It was a woman, somewhat heavy set, and blonde. She turned impatiently, pressing the buzzer again, and he saw her face, recognizing her at once. He sent the elevator down for her.

"Fury Fan," he greeted, as she entered the apartment. "What brings you by?"

"You mean how did I manage to get out of bed this early in the day," she asked. "Funny ain't it, how pretty a city can be at night, and how dumpy it looks in the daylight. Got any coffee?"

"Sure, come on in," he said, genuinely glad to see her.

He led the way to the kitchen. Sophie barked loudly at first, but Jackie introduced them, and after a few sniffs, Sophie decided Fury was there as a friend.

"She's a doll," Fury said, scratching behind Sophie's ears while Jackie poured the coffee.

"Thanks, she seems to like you too." Jackie did not press the question of why Fury was there. He was sure she would explain in her own time.

"I suppose you're wondering why I'm here," she said finally.

"I thought it was all due to my charm," Jackie said with a smile.

She returned the smile. "I already made one pass at you, Junior," she said. "Anyway, you ain't fooling this old bag, I know I ain't got the right fixtures."

"No offense. I just happen to like men," Jackie acknowledged the correctness of her deduction.

"Nothing wrong with that," she said. "I've always had kind of a thing for them myself. That's been my big trouble: every time my britches got warm, they started thinking for me. I was a big star in burlesque, you know, when I was just a kid practically. Had everything going for me. One of the big houses wanted me to sign an exclusive contract, for more money than I could ever have spent. The deal was all set. Then I met this guy who worked as a stagehand. First thing you know, the real show is in my dressing room, not on stage. So we ran away together. That lasted until I found I was headed for motherhood. You can't work as a stripper in that condition. So the lug takes off with the last of my dough."

"What happened to the child?" Jackie asked.

"I lost it. I had to work to eat, and I guess I danced too hard. Nearly killed me too. Might have been better if it had, I guess."

She swallowed a mouthful of coffee. "Well, that's enough of my life and times. I came on business."

"Business?" Jackie was genuinely surprised.

"O. K. and I liked you, I guess you figured that, and we liked what you're doing, trying to catch those dirty dognappers, you know. We talked about it to some of our friends. We still see some of the old gang from time to time, try to stay in touch with one another. Anyway, we felt that we all wanted to help a little, just for the sake of what's right. So we…well, here."

She thrust a small paper bag into his hands. Jackie took it, puzzled, and opened it. There was money inside: a few bills, and a few dollars in coins.

"It ain't much," she said as he stared down into the sack. "But we sort of wanted to help finance what you was doing. I know it won't bring our dog back, of course, or anything like that. But if you can track those SOBs down and put them out of business, it'll save somebody else a lot of grief."

Jackie was deeply touched by the gesture. He knew how much the pitifully few dollars in the sack represented to Fury, O. K., and their "gang." His instinct was to return it, but he knew also that to do so would be to offend the woman before him, and her friends. They had wanted to help in his fight, and this was their best effort—by their standards, a valiant one.

"I don't know what to say, except thanks," he stammered. "This will help, I'm sure. And don't worry, we'll win in this fight. Justice does triumph."

She grunted, and stood. "I ain't so sure of that. But anyway, maybe it'll come in handy."

She cocked her head to one side, listening. Jackie had left the radio playing faintly, and the strains of a song could just be discerned. "Love for Sale," she said, staring into space "I used to sing that one. It was a specialty of mine, if you want to know."

"You must have done it beautifully."

She seemed almost to have forgotten his presence. She hummed a few measures; then, faintly at first, she began to sing. The voice was hoarse and uncertain, and once or twice she paused, screwing up her face as she tried to remember. But it was coming back to her, and as it did, she sang louder and with more confidence.

Jackie listened, enthralled. This was a different Fury Fan, one who, for a moment or so, had stepped into the past. The voice, he was sure, was only a mere shadow of what it had once been, but even so there was magic in the way she sang the song. Maybe, he thought, it was because one knew she had lived what she was singing about. And maybe it was the knowledge that there were very few performers who gave that heartbreaking pathos to their delivery. But whatever it was, it went straight to the heart. There were tears in his eyes as she finished, and his applause was spontaneous.

She seemed suddenly embarrassed to have forgotten herself, and flustered by the applause, although there were tears in her eyes too.

"I guess I'm going a little bats," she sniffed, rummaging in her bag for a handkerchief. "Next thing I'll be stripping on a street corner, or something like that."

"Let me know when you do," he said, following her to the door. "I'd like to catch the show."

She smiled gratefully. As she paused at the elevator, her eyes wandered about the luxurious apartment. He felt almost guilty as he realized she was comparing the elegance of this place with her own cheap rooms.

All she said, though, was, "Nice place."

* * * * * * *

Soon after she had gone, the phone began rang again. It soon became evident that Jackie's newspaper spread was producing results. During the morning, there was a wide variety of phone calls, from newspaper reporters, kennel owners and others in the business, and from people who were simply curious or wanted to tell him about their own pets.

Jackie carefully reported each call to Rich for confirmation of the facts that had been provided. To his disappointment, each seemed to be perfectly above suspicion. He agreed to appointments, none-theless, with all who seemed particularly interested in seeing Sophie. It was quite possible that the dog-nappers might be operating under a perfectly legiti-mate cover, and he wanted to give them every pos-sible opportunity to display their true colors.

As the day wore on, however, it began to seem that his ruse had been unsuccessful. As a wide assortment of visitors came and went, for whom Sophie performed a few of her tricks, Jackie's hopes grew dimmer. Although he was fully alert, he could discern nothing suspicious about any of the callers. All of them seemed to be perfectly innocent people who were genuinely interested in seeing Sophie, the Superdog.

The calls and the visiting traffic had dimin-ished by later afternoon and Jackie was about to call it a day, when he received yet another call, from a man who identified himself as a newspaper reporter for the *Los Angeles Clarion*.

"We'd love an opportunity to interview both you and Sophie," the caller explained. "And to do a story of our own. Would it be possible to make an appointment?"

"Of course, Mister, er...?"

"Harris," the caller supplied the name for him.

"Mister. Harris." Jackie's hopes flared up again. Harris was the name one of the dognappers had given Agatha. It might be a coincidence, or it might be the lead he was waiting for. "I'll be home the rest of the afternoon. Would four-thirty be convenient?"

"I'll be there promptly," Mister Harris informed him.

Jackie eagerly radioed the information to Rich. His excitement mounted when Rich gave him the answer.

"Looks like you might have something," Rich informed him. "There's no such paper as the *Los Angeles Clarion*."

"That's what I suspected," Jackie declared triumphantly. "It has to be them."

"Need any help?" Rich asked. "I can send a couple of the boys over."

"No, I want to take care of these monsters myself," Jackie told him. "If things get out of hand, I can always give you a call."

As he switched off the radio, Jackie could barely suppress his excitement. There was no doubt in his mind that the dognappers had taken the bait, and at least one of them was on his way here right now.

This time, Jackie would be ready for them.

♠ CHAPTER SEVEN ♠
λ

Mister Harris was indeed prompt. He rang the bell at four thirty on the dot. Jackie pushed the button that would set the elevator into operation, and waited to greet his guest. He had to admit to himself that he was curious. Agatha had described Harris as even better looking than Jay, and Jay had certainly been a gorgeous hunk of man.

It took only a glance to assure him that Agatha had not exaggerated. Harris was taller and huskier than Jay had been. He was also golden blond, with skin darkened by the sun to the color of burnished gold. At the moment he wore a very neat suit, but it did not conceal the fine lines of his body, tapering from broad shoulders to slim hips.

"Mr. Holmes?" Harris greeted him as he stepped from the elevator.

"Call me Jackie," Jackie replied, giving the visitor the benefit of one of his most dazzling smiles.

"Thanks, my name is Mark." The smile Harris gave him in return was a dazzling one and disarmingly innocent, but Jackie's shrewd eyes saw the underlying and almost concealed hardness beneath the pleasant facade. Harris created an air of a cheerful, healthy young collegian, but it was apparent that behind that facade he was far from easy going or innocent.

"This is quite a setup," Harris commented. "The elevator is privately controlled?"

"Yes. From inside, it's very simply controlled by this switch." Jackie unhesitatingly displayed the switch to his visitor. He wanted to give Harris all the confidence necessary. Nor did he overlook the fact that Harris' keen eyes made particular note of the switch and its function.

"And this," Harris turned his attention to Sophie. "Must be Superdog."

Another time, Sophie might have treated the visitor more coldly, but she was acting upon Jackie's commands now, greeting each of the day's visitors with warm and innocent affection. She came quickly to Harris' outstretched hand, tail wagging enthusiastically as he petted.

"She certainly looks like an ordinary poodle, doesn't she?" Harris commented, standing again.

"You know the old *cliché* about judging books by their covers, I'm sure," Jackie replied. "But may I suggest a cocktail?"

"I'd love one, if I'm not imposing upon you."

"Not at all, I enjoy charming company." Jackie led the way to the living room. As they entered, Harris paused in front of a long credenza. Atop the piece of furniture was a tall, woodcarving. Erect and highly polished, it was an accurate if enlarged reproduction of a male sexual organ.

"Most unusual," Harris commented.

"A gift," Jackie replied, suppressing a smile. If he had entertained any doubts about Harris' sexual leanings, the appreciative gleam in the young man's eyes would have dispelled them.

"But what are all these scratches?" Harris asked with a puzzled expression. "It looks too well cared for simply to have been marred."

"They're not exactly scratches," Jackie said. "I suppose you could call them notches." He devoted his attention to mixing martinis.

It took Harris a moment to understand. When he did, he grinned broadly. "You must be rather, shall I say, active?" he remarked. "I see there are two brand new marks."

"I keep busy," Jackie handed him a cocktail, pleased to note that Harris had assumed a slightly warmer attitude toward him. "Of course, success is usually dependent upon quality."

"Here's to quality." Harris toasted him with his glass before sipping the drink.

Jackie returned the gesture. Unless he was mistaken, Mister Mark Harris had decided upon his plan of attack. It very much looked as though Jackie were about to be seduced, something he always enjoyed.

"I do hope you're not in a hurry," Jackie said. "I hate rushing things."

"Oh, I have plenty of time. This is quite an apartment." Harris glanced around appreciatively. The apartment was indeed a stunning one, furnished with pieces that were, many of them, literally treasures.

"An unusual collection." Harris had turned to a wall covered with various objects.

"Personal mementos," Jackie explained. "And of course, for that reason, the more valuable to me."

He did not explain that the mementos were in fact souvenirs of his many assignments with C.A.M.P. They were a diverse lot. There was the crest of Castle Gaye, reproduced in sterling silver—that had been presented to him by the Castle's owner, the handsome and fabulous Baron Max Von der Gout. Jackie had labeled that particular file *Gothic Gaye*. It had been a dangerous and spine tingling adventure at the Baron's Castle Gaye, one filled with ghosts and death, and more than a little romance.

Near the silver crest was another memento, even more eye-catching. It appeared to be a stupendously large diamond mounted on a background of blue velvet. It was, as Jackie knew, synthetic, but a devilishly clever imitation that had involved Jackie in another of his closed cases, one he had labeled *The Man from C.A.M.P.* Working with handsome and straight Ted Summers, Jackie had broken up the clever diamond producing ring, but almost at the cost of his life.

Beside the phony diamond, a gold phonograph record seemed almost out of place. It was the sort of record presented to singers whose records have sold a million copies; and in fact, it had been presented to the famed British rock and roll singer, Dingo Stark, for just that reason. But the *Color Him Gay* file had begun with Dingo as the victim of a fiendish blackmail plot, from which the resourceful Jackie had finally managed to rescue him. In gratitude, Dingo had given Jackie the record for his trophy collection—and some more personal expressions of his gratitude as well.

A large jeweled butterfly pin was a remembrance of *The Watercress File.* Jackie smiled as he thought of the madcap bunch, including his spinster aunts, who had formed W.A.T.E.R.C.R.E.S.S., their own espionage organization, but it was with their help that Jackie had foiled an international plot.

Yet another adventure, *The Son Goes Down,* was represented by a certificate that showed Jackie to be a member of the Dean James Fan Club, a membership that had nearly ended Jackie's career and his life, as he had fought to end the activities of a ruthless kidnapping ring who provided pretty young boys to serve as prostitutes in pleasure palaces throughout the world.

Beside that was a blond wig that Jackie had worn in his *Rally Round the Fag* case, when it had been necessary for him to pose as a woman. He had taken the place of a female agent, only to discover that she had a Lesbian lover, a role that Jackie was hardly qualified to play.

There were others, many of them, but Harris, of course, could not know the meaning behind them.

"It's certainly an unusual collection," Harris said again.

"Perhaps you'd like to see some of the rest of the apartment," Jackie offered. "I like to pride myself that it's a little on the unusual side."

"I'd love to," Harris replied enthusiastically.

Jackie led the way back toward the entrance hall, stopping at the door.

"This," he explained. "Lets me see who my visitors are."

He turned on a closed circuit television screen that revealed the vestibule of the building. He was not particularly surprised to see that there were people there at the moment. One of them he was able to recognize immediately: it was handsome Jay Cleland.

It was not hard to guess that the woman with him was the vile creature whom Agatha had described: Anna Lingus. Her wickedly beautiful face was framed by long, straight black hair. She wore a severely cut suit of black leather and her accessories too were black: hat, gloves, shoes, even the elegantly long cigarette holder, tipped with a black cigarette. She looked like nothing quite so much as a black panther, graceful, beautiful, and deadly.

A slight movement cast fleeting shadows. There were others in the vestibule also, but they were out of the camera range. It was apparent that Harris had brought his entire group with him. Nor did Jackie miss the alarm that registered on Harris' face when the group was revealed on the screen.

"They must be visiting someone else in the building," Jackie commented unconcernedly, flicking off the camera. He turned his back on the entrance. "The closets, of course, are operated by power also." Another button brought a guest closet revolving out of what had appeared to be a solid wall.

"The other rooms are through here." At Jackie's touch, another solid wall moved aside, revealing a hallway.

Fascinated, Harris followed him through various rooms: a library which as Jackie pointed out, contained the world's most extensive collection of first editions; an intimate paneled den, and finally, the master bedroom itself, spacious and luxurious.

"Splendid," Harris declared as he surveyed the room. "You actually live like a king."

"Or a queen," Jackie suggested with a laugh. He was eager now to start the action.

Harris did not let the hint go unnoticed. He smiled seductively, fixing soft eyes on Jackie. "You're quite attractive," he said simply.

"So are you." Jackie remained motionless as Harris moved a step closer and embraced him in strong young arms, drawing him against a firm, manly body. Their lips met in a scorching kiss.

"I was hoping you'd do that," Jackie whispered when it had ended.

"I wanted to from the moment I set eyes on you," Harris replied. His large, powerful hands moved urgently over Jackie's slender body. "I've been aflame with desire."

He guided Jackie toward the canopied bed, gently yet firmly. Jackie offered no resistance. He could scarcely help regretting that this was only a game. It would be easy to believe that Harris was sincere, and no more than what he seemed to be, a passionate young man. But Jackie knew the truth, and he knew he dared not let his guard be weakened by soft words and hungry caresses.

They fell across the bed, clinging to one another in a torrid embrace. Harris smothered him with kisses, nibbling at his ears and his throat. It was time, Jackie knew, to set the wheels in motion, but he could not resist the temptation for a brief taste of the pleasures being offered to him. He moved his hand down, finding and easily opening the front of his companion's trousers.

"Nice," he murmured, truthfully. For a moment he freed himself from the arms holding him, moving downward. Harris might be pretending about a great deal, he thought, but there was no doubt that his arousal was genuine.

"I'll be right back," Jackie whispered, forcing himself to get up from the bed.

"Hurry," Harris panted, looking up with smoldering eyes.

Jackie disappeared into the bathroom, closing the door firmly. At the same time, he pushed a concealed button. One wall glowed with light, and hidden cameras gave him a complete view of the bedroom.

For a long moment Harris remained on the bed, half-naked. Even a room away, Jackie could see the struggle that was taking place inside him. On one hand, he clearly desired to finish what they had started on the bed. On the other hand, he could not forget that he had come for a specific purpose.

Inherent evil won. With a frustrated sigh, Harris rose from the bed, pulling up his trousers. With a glance in the direction of the bathroom, Harris moved swiftly and lightly from the room.

Jackie pushed another button, and watched Harris' progress down the hall. As he had suspected, Harris stopped at the elevator controls and pushed the button that would send the elevator down for his cronies. Then he moved on to the living room. Another button gave Jackie a view of that room, as Harris hurried to the chair in which Sophie was dozing.

Sophie was following her instructions to the letter. She offered no protest as Harris picked her up. She even licked his face in gesture of approval.

As the elevator door slid open, Jackie removed his gun from its hiding place. At the flick of a switch, another door opened from the bathroom, directly into the central hall.

The band stealing into the hall from the elevator froze in their tracks as Jackie appeared suddenly before them, gun in hand. Harris, halfway across the living room with Sophie in his arms, froze in his tracks.

"Sophie, attack," Jackie ordered sharply.

The transformation was one certain to strike terror into the heart of the most ruthless criminal. One minute Harris was carrying a harmless ball of white fluff in his arms. The next instant, he was holding a lethal whirlwind. Sophie's teeth closed over his wrist, ripping the skin open. He screamed with pain, jumping back and dropping the dog. Like a flash, Sophie leaped again, this time for his throat. In terror, Harris dodged, trying to avoid the razor sharp fangs that threatened to tear him to shreds.

In the hall, Harris' companions were momentarily at a loss. One of them, a stranger to Jackie, reached for a gun. Jackie fired, and there was a yelp of pain as the bullet struck the man's wrist.

Jackie's gun held only a single shot. As Jay dived for him, Jackie lifted it and brought it crashing down against the man's head. It was a stunning blow, but Jay had the strength of a bull. His charge was scarcely slowed. Jackie was grabbed in arms like bands of steel, thrown back against the wall by the force of the rush.

Jackie summoned all of his strength. He lifted his assailant from the floor, spinning around to crash Jay against the wall. Again, although the blow should have stunned a gorilla, Jay seemed barely discomfited.

Jackie managed to break the hold, struggling to get a grip of his own, but Jay was as fast as he was strong. He ducked, seizing Jackie from behind. Jackie's head was locked in a grip of death.

Anna, her eyes blazing with fury, stepped toward him. In the light of the chandeliers Jackie saw a gleam of metal. In horror he realized that her clever gloves had concealed claws of steel, razor sharp weapons that were even now being raised to slash his face to ribbons. For a fraction of a second he hesitated. It was against his principles to strike a lady. Yet even as that thought crossed his mind, he knew that Anna was no lady. Using Jay's own body as a support, he lifted both feet from the floor and kicked out savagely. His feet caught her in the stomach, sending her hurtling backward, with a cry of pain.

The force of his kick had thrown Jay off balance as well. They crashed to the floor. With a mighty effort, Jackie lunged free of his attacker. With all of the considerable strength that he could muster, he delivered a bone-shattering blow to Jay's chin. This time the blow registered. Jay's eyes rolled dazedly in his head.

Even as he prepared to deliver a final blow and render his opponent unconscious, Jackie's trained nostrils caught a scent that sent a chill through him. With a lightening- like movement, he threw himself aside as a tiny dart shot into the wall. A second later and the dart, tipped with the most deadly of poisons, would have struck him.

The cigarette holder that Anna had carried had become a hideous weapon, a dart gun. He realized now that these were no ordinary wrongdoers he was fighting, but people of ingenious and fiendish methods.

Luck was with him, however. It was clear that Anna had only the one dart, as she hurled the fake cigarette holder at him in blind fury.

"Damn you," she cursed, staring blindly about. Jay was stunned almost to unconsciousness. In the living room, Harris was crashing about the room trying to escape the attack of the demon Sophie. The third man, ignoring his wounded arm, charged toward Jackie, but Jackie sidestepped his clumsy attack with ease and sent the man sprawling across the floor.

The move, however, had given Anna time to act. She grabbed her companion's gun from the floor and, before Jackie could jump for her had it trained on him.

"I'll kill you for this mess," she yelled, her face contorted into a mask of rage. "And your dog, too, unless you call her off."

She turned the gun in Sophie's direction. Jackie knew that she meant what she said and he had no doubt that she was a good shot. She was too far from him to reach her in time to throw off her aim.

"Sophie, stop," Jackie called sharply. Immediately, Sophie froze where she was. The command was just in time to save the life of Mark Harris, who had fallen to the floor, no longer able to ward off her attack.

In that moment of frozen action, the buzzer sounded from below. Her eyes trained on Jackie, Anna pushed the answering buzzer.

"Yes?" she asked sharply.

"It's the police," came the voice from below. "There's a car parked illegally down here, a black sedan. Is it yours?"

"Yes, I'll be down in a few minutes," Anna answered him.

"Sorry, but you'll have to move it right away," the voice on the intercom said, "Or I'll have to put a ticket on it."

She grimaced in frustration. "All right," she snapped sharply. "We're coming."

The disabled band rushed toward the elevator, their only thought now one of escape. Jackie watched helplessly as his enemies escaped his grasp.

"Just to keep you occupied for a moment," Anna called as the door started to close. She hurled a tiny pellet in his direction. Jackie realized too late what it was. Before he could cover his face, the gas had exploded about him. His eyes and nostrils seemed to be afire. Sophie let out a yelp as the burning gas reached her.

Jackie staggered to his feet and lunged toward the elevator, but the gas had given the evil band the time they had needed to make their escape. Even as he pushed the button to stop the elevator, the light above it told him that it had reached the lobby. They would be in their car and gone before he could get downstairs.

He swore aloud as he stumbled toward the room, his eyes still burning. Anna and her cronies had won this round, but the fight was not yet over.

The Man from C.A.M.P.

♠ CHAPTER EIGHT ♠
λ

Cold towels on their eyes helped relieve him and Sophie of their discomfort, at least physically. It was a despondent Jackie however who called Rich to report the results of his efforts.

"Damn," Rich swore, "I knew I should have been there. Are you all right?"

"Nothing but a few bruises," Jackie assured him. "And a bad temper. Underestimating one's enemy is the worst mistake any agent can make. Now I have to start all over again."

Having completed his report, Jackie turned his attention to the apartment. The living room was in shambles, the result of Harris' frenzied efforts to escape Sophie. Jackie set himself to putting it in order again.

He had scarcely begun his task when the door buzzer sounded. To his surprise, it was Don's handsome face that greeted him from the screen.

I was in the area," his red headed friend explained. "And I thought I'd drop in."

Jackie glanced around at the disorder, but he did not want to offend his attractive and satisfying playmate. "Come on up," he said, pushing the button to send down the elevator.

"To be honest," Don explained when he arrived upstairs, "I read that newspaper account about your incredible dog, and I was dying of curiosity to see her."

He paused as he saw the evidence of the fight that had taken place a short time before. "What happened here?" he asked, bewildered.

"Just a little disagreement between friends," Jackie told him. He saw his derringer where it had fallen on the floor and bent to pick it up.

"Some friends," Don said. "Are you sure there isn't something you haven't told me about yourself?"

Jackie grinned ruefully. "I guess I may as well explain about myself, now that we're better acquainted. Let's have a drink, though, shall we?"

* * * * * * *

When they had seated themselves with the drinks, Jackie explained briefly about C.A.M.P., and his association with it.

"You mean you're a secret agent?" Don was astonished. "I'd never have suspected it."

"I'm not sure that's a compliment, but I guess it is," Jackie said with a laugh.

"And Sophie," Don petted the dog's head. "She's an agent too? No wonder you said she was so valuable. She must be worth a fortune."

"Yes she is," Jackie agreed. "And she nearly fell into the hands of those dognappers. They'd have me at their mercy in that case."

"The dognappers? But of course, you must be working on that case now. No wonder you were so interested in what happened to Lady Agatha's dog."

"Yes, I've been trying to catch them at work. I nearly succeeded, too." He explained about his attempts to break the ring, concluding with a description of the scene that had taken place earlier in the apartment.

"Good Heavens, you might have been killed," Don exclaimed, shocked.

"That's a possibility those of us who work for C.A.M.P. rarely consider," Jackie said sincerely. "The important thing is catching our prey."

"It sounds as though they've outfoxed you," Don pointed out.

"Only for the moment. But don't worry," Jackie said, "I already have an idea. In fact, I can even use your help."

"My help?" Don was surprised. "I'd love to, of course. I think it's all very exciting. But how can I help?"

"Just by having a few drinks with me."

"A few drinks?" Don looked puzzled.

Jackie nodded, the plan already falling into place in his mind. "Yes. After that fight today, those people will probably rest tonight. But they'll be back in business by tomorrow, you can bet on it. I'm going to use Sophie as a decoy again, and see if they're still using the method of stealing dogs from outside the gay bars."

"But won't they recognize you?" Don asked. "If they see you in a bar, they're sure to guess that it's a trick."

"Not if I'm in disguise. Don't worry, I mastered that art as a part of my training. I'm certain they won't know who I am."

"What about Sophie?"

Jackie grinned. "We'll disguise her too. A little black dye, and they'll never know it's the same dog. Then we'll make the rounds of some of the bars, leaving Sophie in the car. If they're out prowling, they're bound to spot her, and try to steal her."

"What then?"

"I'll have the car wired, so that as soon as they try to break into it, I'll receive a signal inside the bar."

"Isn't that taking a chance? What if they manage to get her and escape before you can get out of the bar and to the car?"

"Not with Sophie," Jackie said. "Believe me, she'll see to it that they're delayed, long enough for me to reach them."

"It sounds like it might work," Don agreed thoughtfully.

"It must work. These people can't be allowed to continue their nefarious crimes. But it will be more effective if I have someone else with me when I hit the bars. We'll look like two ordinary lovers, out for a few drinks."

"I'm game," Don said with a grin. "I still say it sounds pretty exciting. Anyway, I haven't been in a good fight for years."

"You may get one. But just to be safe, I'll see that you're armed. I can't give you a lethal gun of course, but I can give you one that fires very special bullets. They're harmless, but contain a powerful drug that will put anyone sound asleep instantly."

Don grinned eagerly at the prospect of so much excitement. "I only wish it were tonight instead of tomorrow night," he said. "I'm ready to go now."

Jackie smiled and leaned closer, resting one hand on a husky thigh. "I'm sure we can find some way to pass the evening, if we really put our heads to it."

"I think we could put more than our heads to it," was the reply.

They stood and made their way to the bedroom. Jackie felt a passing sensation of guilt as he realized that he had been thinking back to Mark Harris. His desire for that young man was still with him, but he slipped an arm around Don's waist. A small part of his desires might have sprung from another source, but he had no lack of desire for his companion.

In the bedroom, they quickly shed their clothes, and found their way to the bed, relaxing for a moment in one another's arms. Jackie sighed with pleasure as Don's hands began gently to stroke his body. His flesh stirred as the strokes became more fervent, gradually moving lower. His own hand moved, across a firm, flat stomach, slipping downward through the coarse garland of red hair.

It was funny, he thought, as their hands began to move in unison, slowly but with increasing speed. This dognapping case was as bad a one as he bad been involved in, yet from it had sprung his friendship with this beautiful young creature.

He turned, offering Don his lips. He felt the burning tip of Don's tongue moving into his mouth, seeking out his. Jackie's hand moved down a muscular back, over the hard-soft flesh of buttocks as white as snow, into the downy crevice that separated them

"I hope you saved that for me," he whispered to Don.

"Ummm hmmmm. Kept it on ice, if you must know."

Jackie chuckled, remembering his previous evening with Don. It had been interesting, but tonight he needed no oddities to fire his imagination.

They shifted positions, Don turning until his back was to Jackie, and they lay on their sides. Jackie guided himself slowly to the object of his desires. There was the laborious interval as entry was gained slowly; then Jackie felt himself again embraced by warm, surrendering flesh.

He began, gently at first, to thrust, his hips, moving to and fro in a gradually widening arc. By this time, all thoughts of Mark Harris had vanished from his mind. For the moment, there were no dognappers, no C.A.M.P., no case to be solved—only the full, yielding buttocks thrusting back against his body.

* * * * * * *

Lady Agatha shifted the packages in his arm as he waited for the light to change. It had been a busy morning, but an enjoyable one, as shopping excursions into Hollywood invariably were. He had managed, after what seemed an eternity of shopping, to find just the right sweater, and suede slacks too. So sexy, he was almost sorry he hadn't worn them when he left the store. Heaven alone knew who might stop him on the street and want to feel them.

Not only had he found all these divine clothes, but with his typical audacity, he had managed to collect an interesting supply of new telephone numbers as well. The sales clerk in the sweater shop for one—such a gorgeous fanny, and so friendly. And that cute little busboy, hanging to his knees, at the restaurant where he'd had lunch. That one had been a little more difficult. Now who would have thought of floating a note in a cup of coffee? Very ingenious, that one.

The light changed at last. With his eyes following the progress of a pair of diminutive buttocks encased in navy whites, Agatha made his way across the street. On the opposite side, the sailor turned to his left. Agatha hesitated. The young tar was awfully cute. But he was just beat from all the shopping, and he had been on his way to the Golden Saucer for coffee, just three doors down, and to the right.

With a last wistful look after the white-garbed ass, Agatha turned to the right, and made his way to the coffee shop. He frowned as he entered. The place was crowded. That made for good cruising, but didn't do a thing for his aching feet.

"Maybe I know someone sitting in one of the booths," he thought, "And can get myself invited to sit down."

He moved to the side of the shop on which the booths were located, and glanced up and down the length of the room.

Luck was with him. His eyes brightened as he recognized the redhead seated about halfway down the length of the shop. It was Don, that adorable little redhead from the Westgate, the one he had met the night Cynthia had been stolen. Too bad, he thought as he started in that direction, that that evening had been so disastrous. He had been just positive that he was on the verge of snatching that one from under Jackie's nose, a victory in the never ended but friendly competition the two of them had engaged in so long as they had known one another.

Agatha had almost reached Don's booth before he saw the young man seated with Don. He recognized him at once, and the recognition was sufficient to freeze him in his tracks.

There was no mistake about it, either. He was not likely to forget Mark Harris so quickly. After all, one didn't meet dognappers every day in the week.

He searched his mind for some explanation. Coincidence? An accidental meeting? Perhaps they had known each other at some time in the past? But as he watched the two, there was no doubt that they knew each other well, this was clearly more than just casual acquaintance.

Whatever it meant—and figuring out the answer to that question out was a job for someone more experienced than he was—one thing was certain: this was something Jackie should know. Agatha turned, forgetting entirely his aching feet, and hurried again toward the door.

110

The front end of the shop was one large, mirrored wall that reflected virtually the entire room. Agatha instinctively glanced into the mirror, his eyes seeking the booth in which the puzzling duo was seated. At the same instant, Don looked up. The look of recognition and surprise was recognizable, even at the distance. Agatha dropped his eyes at once. Maybe, he thought hopefully as he hurried out of the door, he hadn't really been recognized. No, he was certain Don had recognized him, but maybe Don would not realize that he had been seen and recognized.

On the sidewalk outside, he hesitated. There were no phone booths visible in the immediate area. He thought of his car, in a lot, only three blocks away. Deciding on that course of action, he started toward the parking lot.

He was almost there when an older model Ford pulled up to the curb beside him, horn blaring. Agatha recognized Don again as he turned to look. This time Don was alone, and waving to him. There was nothing he could do but step from the curb, to the open window of the car.

"Thought I recognized you," Don greeted him.

"Where did you see me?" Agatha asked, trying to play dumb.

"Where? Why, right here, of course, what do you mean?"

Agatha was flustered. His question had been a stupid one. Don was certain now to suspect that Agatha had seen him before.

"I just thought...oh, I'm not thinking clearly, I guess."

"Come on, I'll give you a lift," Don said with a seemingly innocent smile.

Agatha hesitated for several seconds. He wanted desperately to contact Jackie, and pass on his discovery. But he was frightened now, and certain that, if he refused the offer, Don would be even more suspicious. If Don were involved with the dognappers, then he was as ruthless as they. There was no telling what he might do, even here on a busy street.

Attempting to seem friendly and very nonchalant, Agatha opened the door and slid into the car. His hands were trembling as they pulled away from the curb.

"Your place?" Don asked.

"Oh, I guess so." Agatha found himself simply unable to think clearly. If he asked to go the parking lot only a few feet away, that would make his getting into the car seem the more questionable. Oh dear, he was thinking, this business of crime fighting must be an awfully complicated one. What on earth would Jackie do in this situation?

It was at least flattering that Don remembered the way to Agatha's apartment without any prompting, although at the moment even that fact served to further unnerve Agatha.

"I could use some coffee," Don said as he parked in front of Agatha's place. "Believe it or not, I haven't had any yet this morning."

Agatha came very close to pointing out that he did not believe it, and explaining why. Instead, he ran a hand wearily across his forehead. "I'd love to invite you in, but I've so much to get done this morning."

"Funny," Don said, staring strangely at him. Almost, Agatha thought, right through him. "I would have sworn you were interested in me."

Agatha managed a small laugh and a flick of his hand. "Don't be silly, darling, of course I am."

Don relaxed and grinned. "Well, then let's go," he said, opening the door on his side.

Feeling increasingly trapped, Agatha led the way to his apartment. Inside, he dropped his parcels on one end of the sofa.

"Have a seat," he suggested. "I'll make some coffee."

Don dropped a hand meaningfully to his crotch, and rubbed. "Coffee isn't really essential," he said in a husky voice.

Agatha swallowed hard. "Well, I think I could use some myself," he managed to stammer. "I'll only take a minute."

He vanished into the kitchen, careful to close the door after himself. He hurried straight to the extension telephone there and began, with shaking hands, to dial Jackie's number.

His dialing stopped abruptly as the door swung open, and Don stepped into the kitchen. His easy-going, flirtatious manner was gone. He looked as hard and vicious now as the dognappers whom Agatha had encountered before.

"Ordering coffee sent in?" Don asked in, a voice of ice.

"No, I just remembered I, I have to call a friend," Agatha stammered.

"Oh. Well, go ahead, don't let me interrupt." Don leaned against one wall, arms folded over his chest.

Agatha replaced the receiver in the cradle. "I guess it isn't that important. I'll make that coffee instead."

"You saw me with him, didn't you?" Don asked. His eyes caught and held Agatha's.

"With Mark Harris? No, of course...." Agatha caught himself, but it was too late. He saw the nasty grin that spread over his companion's face.

Agatha's eyes widened in terror as Don slowly pulled a switchblade knife from his pocket. With a click, the blade sprang into view.

"Looks like I'm going to have to take care of you," Don said calmly as he started across the room. "Before you get to finish that call."

* * * * * * *

The following evening, Don arrived at Jackie's apartment promptly at nine o'clock, as they had agreed. He was puzzled, as he first stepped out of the elevator and into the apartment, to see an absolute stranger before him, and no sign of Jackie. His surprise was followed quickly by belated recognition, however, and astonishment.

"Jackie, is it really you?" he asked.

Jackie grinned and nodded. "In the flesh," he said. "I guess that means my disguise is effective."

Indeed, it would have been difficult to recognize him as the same individual. In place of the fair, blond appearance that was usual to him, he had become a dark-haired, dark-skinned Latin. His hair was black and curly, worn slightly long as a concession to the current styles. His eyebrows too were black, and cosmetic contact lenses had changed the

114

color of his eyes to an indeterminate dark shade. His skin was now an olive hue that looked Mediterranean. But he had changed his features as well, using C.A.M.P.'s highly advanced materials and techniques to broaden his nose and give his face a rounder, fuller appearance.

"It's phenomenal," was Don's conclusion. "If I hadn't walked in here expecting to see you, I'm certain I'd never have recognized you for yourself."

"And this," Jackie said as a dark creature ran to them. "Is our little Sophie."

Don laughed as he swept Sophie up into his arms. The fluffy white poodle had also become a dark-haired beauty. "It's perfect. They'll never guess that you two are the same pair they tangled with yesterday."

"I'm hoping for that," Jackie answered. He produced a small revolver from his pocket. "This is for you," he said. "It shoots like any ordinary gun. The only difference is that, as I explained yesterday, the bullets won't harm them at all, merely put them immediately to sleep. Use it only as a necessity."

They took the elevator to the garage, where the car Jackie had selected was waiting for them.

"You've changed cars," Don commented, noting that this was not the same fabulous vehicle Jackie had driven previously, but a rather ordinary little MG sports roadster.

"Had to. For one thing, there's a possibility they might have seen the other one the day I was at their house. For another thing, they'd never be able to break into the other one. I want them to think they're dealing with an ordinary pair of homosexuals, until the showdown."

Jackie had decided previously what bars they should visit. Intuition told him that the best results might be obtained at the Westgate, where Agatha's dog had been stolen, but there were several similar bars on the way there, in out of the way locations and on less traveled streets, and he had decided to check them out as well.

At the first one, he deliberately parked off the main street, on a dark side street where the dognappers would feel safe in breaking into the car without any great risk of being seen by passing motorists.

Inside, the crowd was still small. It would not grow large until much later in the evening. The bar was decorated in a mock Yukon style, including billboards from early movies and plays like The Gold Rush and The Pride of the Mounties. A large player piano provided the accompaniment for a handful of young men who stood around it, singing show tunes in loud and rather unmusical voices. Jackie and Don ordered beers and joined them. Jackie had suggested to Don that they pretend to be a couple, but it was not a hard act for them to keep up. They exchanged frequent glances, smiles, and discreet touches.

By the time they had finished their beers, nothing had happened, and Jackie suggested to Don that they go. There were several disappointed glances in their direction as they made their way from the bar. Sophie was waiting patiently in the car, jumping up to the window as she saw them approaching.

"As a matter of curiosity," Don asked when they were on their way again, "How will you know if they do try to get Sophie out of the car?"

"That was easy," Jackie said. "The windows are wired to an alarm signal. To get in, they'll have to smash a window. That will set off a small buzzer on my watch, just loud enough for me to hear it, but not loud enough to attract anyone else's attention. After that, I have to depend upon Sophie to delay them, for about a minute; just long enough for us to get outside."

Their next stop was at an unobtrusive little bar called the West Addition. It was a long, narrow place, filled with a younger crowd of patrons. Some of them were playing pool in the rear, others stood at the bar, carefully looking over each newcomer.

Again the visit was uneventful. Disappointed, they tried yet another spot, the Coach and Four. This was a combined bar and small restaurant, and offered a slightly more fashionable interior, with paintings on the walls and a number of patrons in suits and ties. Regrettably, it was as uneventful as the others.

"Well, let's see if lightning strikes in the same place twice," Jackie suggested as they started out for the Westgate. Once there, he circled about until he found a parking place almost in the same spot where Agatha's car had been parked on the previous occasion. If the dognappers were in the area, he wanted to offer them every temptation to repeat their good fortune.

* * * * * * *

As usual, the Westgate was not terribly crowded. They ordered beers and sat at the bar. A few people came and went, some of whom greeted

Jackie briefly. The tiny alarm in Jackie's watch remained silent, however.

As they finished their beers, Jackie felt the need to visit the restroom in the rear. He hesitated, however, as he thought of Sophie and their reason for being here. If the alarm sounded while he was in the restroom, he would be giving the dognappers an extra minute or so of operation. He glanced in Don's direction, and the answer came to him.

"I'm going to the restroom," he said, slipping the watch from his wrist. "And I want you to wear this for a few minutes. If anything happens, give me a yell at once."

As he, stood from the stool, he caught sight of a man at the far end of the bar, one he had scarcely noticed before because the man was seated in a dark area. Jackie's breath caught in his throat as he recognized the man. He had been with Anna and Jay at his apartment the day before, the one with the gun. So the dognappers were in the area.

He made his way to the restroom, deciding to make his visit a brief one. As he passed the man at the end of the bar, something stirred in Jackie's mind, but the thought eluded him before he could grasp it and bring it to light.

Inside the restroom, the thought came to him again. He had seen that man before, not only yesterday at his apartment, but earlier, here in this very bar. It was the same man who had sent drinks to Agatha and Don the night Agatha's dog had been stolen. Was there any significance in that fact? Puzzled, and suddenly apprehensive, Jackie hurried from the restroom, but the man was gone.

Don was standing at the jukebox, in the act of selecting some records. Jackie walked to him.

"That didn't take long," Don commented.

"I had something on my mind. Did you...?" He suddenly stopped. "Don, the watch!"

Jackie's keen ears had caught a faint buzzing sound. His eyes went to Dan's wrist, but the redhead had thrust his hand into his pocket as he stood. The faint ringing of the alarm was almost inaudible.

At Jackie's words, Don glanced at his hand in dismay. When he yanked his hand from the pocket, the buzzing became more distinct.

"Oh, damn," he exclaimed. "I forgot."

"Come on," Jackie said, dashing for the door. Don was only a few feet behind him.

The street seemed still as they rounded the corner, heading toward the spot where the car had been parked. Jackie caught a glimpse of a car, without any lights, rounding a corner in the distance.

He could see long before he reached his car, that the windows had been smashed open. In horror, he realized that Sophie was gone, and the car empty.

"Oh God," Don gasped as they ran up to the car. "And it's my fault for being so careless. I just didn't think...."

Jackie stared in the direction in which the car he had seen had vanished. "It's peculiar," he said. "We couldn't have lost more than a minute through that mistake. Sophie should have delayed them for that long, unless...."

He leaned over and thrust his head through the shattered window, sniffing. "Gas, sleeping gas," he exclaimed. "They fired a gas pellet through the broken window, and knocked her out cold."

He stared for a moment at the empty interior of the, car. "But why would they have done that, unless they already knew who she was, and how dangerous she was? Surely they couldn't have recognized her."

"They must have, despite the disguise." Don was despondent. "And now they have her as their prisoner, and it's my fault. They've outsmarted us."

"Not entirely," Jackie declared, suddenly realizing that he was wasting precious seconds. He ran around the car, to the driver's side. "I took a few precautions, just in case anything went wrong."

Don paused for a moment, puzzled.

"Get in, hurry" Jackie snapped, starting up the engine.

"But what can we do?" Don asked, doing as he had been ordered. "They have too much of a head start for us to find them now."

"That's what they think," Jackie replied. "What they don't know is that I planted a homing device on Sophie, so that they could never find it, taped to the skin beneath her collar. With the receiver I installed in this car, we'll have no trouble tracking them."

As he spoke, he pulled open an unobtrusive panel on the dash, to reveal a tracking screen. The red light moving across it pinpointed the location of the getaway car. With one eye on the screen, Jackie followed the path of the dognappers. The villains had a head start on him, but he could count on the fact that they considered themselves safe from pursuit. They would not be attempting to lose him.

120

"Then you can follow them right to their hideout?" Don asked, also watching the tracking screen.

"That's right," Jackie replied. "And this time I'm prepared for the full bag of tricks."

He drove swiftly and skillfully. The red dot on the screen was growing larger in size. He was drawing closer.

"I'm afraid there's one trick you overlooked," Don said calmly beside him.

Jackie glanced in his companion's direction, and found himself staring down the wrong end of the gun he had given Don.

"You?" Jackie exclaimed, understanding at once. "You're one of them?"

"Of course," Don answered with a smug grin.

As Jackie recovered from the shock, he began to put the pieces of the puzzle together. As he did so, Don's part in the adventure began to make sense.

"Then it was you who found me with Jay," he said. "And knocked me out."

"That's right. I didn't know anything about C.A.M.P. then, or your work, but I was suspicious, and when I came in and saw you in bed with Jay, I was sure it was more than just a coincidence, so I put you to sleep. Jay wanted to kill you right then, in case you were curious, but I thought it would be best to wait until we knew more about you. That's why I was so friendly with you."

"And it was your job to distract your victims, while your friends stole the dogs."

"That night you met me, my partner came in and sent beers to Agatha and me. That meant that

Agatha had left a dog in the car, and I was to keep him occupied until they had time to steal the dog,"

"And the night I came to your apartment, you were so passionate," Jackie said. "Every time I got ready to leave, you coaxed me into staying longer. But that was all an act."

"Well, not entirely. I was enjoying myself immensely," Don said, "But you had mentioned having a valuable dog, and you had given me the address. My friends went there to steal the dog, but of course, they couldn't get in."

"So they tried again?"

"And failed. After that, Anna swore she'd get that dog from you, and make you pay for the trouble you'd caused."

"And I played right into your hands tonight," Jackie said despondently. "You deliberately ignored that signal, giving your friends time to break into the car. And of course that's how they knew who she was, and to use sleeping gas on her."

"So now you know it all." Don seemed quite proud of himself. If he experienced any regrets over his deceit, they were not apparent.

"And now what?" Jackie risked a glance at the screen. They were quite near the dognappers by this time, within a block or so.

"Now I'm going to let my friends know about that homing device, so that you can't sneak up on us. Then you're going to share a generous portion of that vast fortune of yours, with us. That is, if you expect to see that dog of yours alive again."

Jackie shuddered involuntarily. He knew the threat was not an idle one. They would not hesitate to kill Sophie if their greedy plans were thwarted. His only chance was to somehow overpower Don.

"We've caught up with your friends," he said aloud, catching sight of taillights before them.

Don glanced through the windshield. For a second his eyes were off Jackie. Jackie seized his opportunity. His foot flew to the brake pedal, slamming it to the floor. The car screeched to a stop, flinging them both forward.

As he was thrown toward the windshield, Don fired, but the bullet missed Jackie. Before he could fire again, Jackie had lunged across the seat.

Don was not the fighter that Jay had been. One blow left him out cold, slumped against the door of the car. Jackie left him where he was, and again slid under the wheel. The brief struggle had given his prey time to pull away from him again. At the moment, his first thought was to catch them. He raced after them once more.

He soon spotted their car again. This time he wasn't going to take a chance on their escaping him. He roared toward them, and shot about them. Grimly he inched his car toward theirs, ignoring the blast from their horn.

Slowly he forced them toward the curb. With one hand he drew his Derringer from his pocket, ready for the moment of confrontation.

They were on a little-traveled side street, with no traffic to interfere with the struggle, but ahead of him he saw the lights of other cars. They were approaching a busy street. The traffic light at the intersection before them changed red.

Desperately, Jackie tried again to force them off the street. The fenders scraped, the cars swerving as they bounced off one another. Jackie's light roadster was at a disadvantage against the large sedan they were driving. The MG bounced and veered nearly out of control. Jackie managed to get in front of them, in their lane, but as he tried to stop for the light, they struck his rear fender with a loud crash, sending him hurtling through the intersection.

With a squeal of tires, the dognappers careened around the corner, just missing another car. Jackie, halfway through the cross street, tried to turn also, but he was unable to dodge the oncoming traffic. There was a tremendous crash as another vehicle collided with him, sending him hurtling across two lanes, to plow into a utility pole.

For a moment he sat stunned; then, in despair, he tried to start the car again, but he knew it was a futile gesture. Ignoring the blood that was pouring from a cut on his arm, he jumped from the car, but the sedan he had been pursuing was already out of sight. They had again escaped him.

He climbed back into the car and leaned across the seat to Don. Even before he felt for a pulse, he knew that the redhead's dognapping days were over. The crash had been fatal for Don.

But his cohorts had made good their escape, and they had Sophie. Jackie turned to the tracking screen, but that hope was quickly dashed. The instrument had been ruined in the crash. The screen was shattered, and the lights out.

Once again his enemies had escaped his grasp.

124

♠ CHAPTER NINE ♠
λ

Nearly an hour had passed by the time Jackie finished with the police and the accident. Fortunately, witnesses had seen the dognappers' car strike his and send him hurtling through the intersection. Luckily, too, no one had been injured in that car that had collided with his. At last Jackie was able to take a cab back to his apartment. He stayed only long enough to replace the makeshift bandage he had applied to his arm, and to transfer his phone calls to the C.A.M.P. office. Then he headed for the office.

Grimly he explained to Rich what had occurred, and that the dognappers had managed to escape him again.

"And they have Sophie, which gives them the upper hand," Rich remarked.

"If they harm her, they will live to regret it," Jackie stated angrily.

"Easy." Rich placed a calming hand on his shoulder. "We have to remain calm if we're going to come up with a solution to this."

"You're right." Jackie forced himself to control his emotions. He could not afford to be anything but clearheaded. He was dealing with enemies of diabolical cleverness, and they were as ruthless as they were wily.

"I think it's safe to assume they'll make the next move," Rich decided after a moment's thought. "They don't want Sophie for herself, but for the ransom they hope to get. They know you're wealthy, and they know Sophie is virtually priceless. I don't think we'll have long to wait before we hear from them."

His hunch was confirmed soon after when the phone rang. The two short rings were a signal that the call was placed to Jackie's home phone and had been automatically transferred here.

He recognized Anna's voice at once. Even before she spoke, she chuckled softly, a sneering, triumphant laugh.

"You fiend," Jackie snarled. "If you've harmed that dog I'll see that you pay."

She laughed again, mockingly. "As a matter of fact, darling, you have that turned around. It's you who must pay. How much is your little monster worth to you?

As Jackie spoke, he was aware that Rich had hurried from the room. Every call that came into this office was automatically traced. He knew that, from the inner room, Rich would be learning the phone number from which Anna was calling.

"You know Sophie is worth any price to me," he said into the receiver, determined to keep her on the phone long enough for Rich to learn her location.

"Yes, I gathered that. But I'm a reasonable woman," Anna said. "I don't want to leave you penniless. Why don't we make it a modest figure, say two hundred and fifty thousand, in cash?"

Jackie gasped aloud. He had expected something outrageous but this was incredible. "That's a quarter of a million dollars," he managed to reply. "You can't be serious."

"But I am, sweets. I want it in cash, and I want it promptly."

"It takes time to gather that much cash."

"From all indications, I should say your resources are rather unlimited. I'm afraid I can only give you until tomorrow."

Jackie hesitated for a moment. With his own resources, and those of C.A.M.P., there was no question that he could raise the money. But he bitterly resented being at the mercy of this heartless woman.

"I haven't got all day," she snapped. "Is it a deal?"

"How do I get you the money?" For the moment, he had no choice but to yield to her demands.

"That's better. You know where Lafayette Park is, don't you?"

"Yes."

"Be in front of the library there tomorrow at noon," she instructed him. "Have the money, and be alone. Do you understand that? Absolutely alone. If there's any foolishness on your part, your dog will die, and it won't be quick, either."

"When will I get her back?"

"When I have the money, and have had a chance to see that you played no tricks. Don't worry, if everything goes my way, I'll see that she's delivered safely back to you. Any other questions, or do we have deal?"

"It's a deal," Jackie said. "But there's something you don't know about. Don was with me when I crashed earlier. Thanks to your nefarious schemes, he's dead."

"Pity." She sounded totally unmoved. "But that's of no consequence now. I'll see you tomorrow." With that she broke the connection.

Rich returned to the room as Jackie replaced the receiver. "No good," he said before Jackie could even ask. "I traced it all right, but the call came from a pay phone in Hollywood. She wasn't taking any chances."

"Did you hear her demands?"

Rich nodded. "I can have the money ready by then, of course. But how do you intend to stop her from getting away with this?"

Jackie was thoughtful for a moment. "We'll have to do as she says, for the moment. But she doesn't know you, or anything about you. There's no reason why you can't be there also, ready to follow her after she picks up the money."

"You're right. I could tail her, and keep you posted as to where we go. Once she leads us to her hideout, we can both move in on them."

"It's taking a chance. If they're forewarned, they'll carry out their threats against Sophie."

"Which means we'll have to be extremely careful." Rich was no less attached to Sophie than Jackie was, and equally determined to see the dognappers brought to justice.

Jackie moved as though to stand, and swayed slightly. Rich jumped up and came to him at once, steadying him.

"Easy," he said. "You've been through a lot. Better try to get some rest."

Jackie wanted to protest, but he knew Rich was right. He had been getting by on a minimum of sleep, going at a heavy pace all the while. The accident in the car had left him battered and bruised. His arm throbbed with a dull ache where it had been hurt.

"I just want to be doing something," he said wearily.

"The best thing you can do is get some rest. You'll want to be on your toes tomorrow."

As he spoke, Rich gathered Jackie easily up into his arms, lifting him as though he weighed only a few ounces.

Jackie relaxed in the strong arms, leaning his bead against the powerful chest. His nostrils were filled with the naturally masculine scent of Rich's body. He closed his eyes as Rich carried him effortlessly to the bedroom, placing him gently across the soft bed.

Rich removed Jackie's clothes quickly and expertly. While Jackie drifted half asleep, half awake, Rich brought towels and warm water, and tenderly bathed his body. He put a fresh dressing on Jackie's wounded arm, and finally he treated Jackie to a skilled massage.

"Asleep?" Rich's deep voice asked in his ear.

"Almost," Jackie managed to murmur. He was turned over on his back. In his floating world of half-consciousness, he was barely aware of the naked flesh that brushed against his. He stirred slightly as he felt Rich's familiar mouth on his crotch, working artfully upon his rapidly engorging flesh.

His body responded mechanically. The tensions of the past few hours contributed to his arousal. His hips rose and fell, lazily at first and then with mounting intensity. He seemed to be soaring upward, floating over the room. His entire awareness was concentrated on that one erect area of his body. It seemed as though his very life-blood were being drawn there, coming together at that point in one massive, throbbing force. Then, sobbingly, he reached the climax of his passion, his hands falling down to grasp at the thick dark hair of Rich's head, pinning him close against his body until the storm of sensation had passed. As it went, his consciousness went with it. Relieved and drained of his frustration and unhappiness, he fell suddenly and totally into a deep sleep.

When he was sure Jackie was asleep, Rich rose from the bed. He stood for a moment, smiling affectionately down at the still young form. For many years he had dreamed of the day when he and Jackie would be free to love one another as two ordinary gay men. Even as he admitted the impossibility of that dream to himself, he still clung to it.

Satisfied that he had completed his work there for the moment, he donned his silk robe and stole quietly from the room, making his way to the inner office that was his domain. There, surrounded by the complex and highly sophisticated equipment that served as his special tools against crime, he began the arrangements for the following day.

A call to High Camp assured him that the money needed for the ransom would be delivered, in cash, within a few hours. His request was not questioned. As an employee of C.A.M.P., his loyalty and honesty were taken for granted, and such a request was assumed to be made as a necessity.

It was also necessary for him to arrange to have the office monitored during his absence the next day, leaving him free to go with Jackie.

At last, satisfied that he had done all that he could do, he returned to the bedroom. Slipping out of the robe, he joined Jackie on the bed, careful in his movements not to disturb his friend's slumber.

Ever so carefully, he lifted Jackie's head and gently placed Jackie within the protective embrace of his arms. Then, with the golden hair falling across his brawny shoulder and his rough hand cupped full of delicious round warmness, he too slept.

THE MAN FROM C.A.M.P.

♠ CHAPTER TEN ♠
λ

Jackie awoke in the morning to the scent of fresh coffee. He opened his eyes and looked up to see Rich standing before him, a steaming cup in his hand.

"Try this," Rich suggested, offering him the cup.

Jackie smiled gratefully and he accepted the brew. As he sat up, his face was almost against his friend's thighs. He was treated to a rather splendid view of Rich's naked and awesome charms.

"Seems to me I owe you something," he commented, reaching out to place a kiss on the warm flesh.

"No hurry," Rich answered, running his hand through Jackie's blond hair. "The longer you wait to pay me back, the more interest I can charge."

"I'd say you've got quite a bit of my interest already," Jackie quipped as the flesh stirred and grew slightly rigid against his lips. But Rich was right, he knew. At the moment, they had work to do. Their pleasure must come later.

They exchanged smiles, and Rich began to dress as Jackie sipped the hot coffee. He had slept late. It was nearly eleven o'clock. In an hour, he had to be ready to match wits again with Anna and her cronies.

"The money's already here," Rich commented. "It was delivered a few hours ago. I counted it, just to be sure." He pointed, as he spoke, to a large suitcase sitting near the bed.

Jackie finished the last of the coffee, and made his way to the bathroom.

A long shower erased the vestiges of sleep. His arm was still a little sore, but aside from that, he was perfectly rested and ready for action.

By the time he had dressed, Rich was waiting for him in the other room. Jackie helped himself to more coffee.

"This is how I see it," he began. "I'll leave here by myself and go to the library as she ordered. You'll bring another car and drive there alone. Park somewhere near the library, so that you can see me, and can see when I hand the money over. Then you'll follow whoever picks up the money. As soon as she leaves me, I'll beat it to my car, and pick you up on the radio."

"Once she's led me to their hideout, I'll wait for you," Rich said.

"We'll have to wait until we get there, and see the house, before we decide what to do next. It may be impossible to get inside without warning them." He did not mention the penalties if they failed.

It was time to go. Grimly, Jackie set out. He went first to his apartment where he picked up his special car. This time he wanted to be prepared for any eventuality. He took time also to change the setting on his phone, so that any calls would be transferred to his car. Then he headed in the direction of Lafayette Park.

The park was near the downtown area of Los Angeles. Both the park and the area were somewhat unsavory, and notorious for the homosexuals who frequented the area, and the scavengers who preyed upon them: stud hustlers, blackmailers, vice officers with the Los Angeles Police Department.

It was only a few minutes before twelve when he arrived. As he hurried down the walk that led to the library, he saw a car that he recognized as one of C.A.M.P.'s. Rich was there already, seated inconspicuously in his car. Several of the cars along the street had people in them, some of them cruising the passing parade in the park, others eating their lunches or reading papers. Engrossed as he seemed to be in a book, Rich was unlikely to cause any concern on the dognappers' part. Jackie passed within a few feet of Rich's car, but neither of them showed any recognition of the other.

Jackie stopped directly in front of the library, the suitcase on the walk before him. He was visible from the park, and from the street that ran along it. If Anna arrived, she could not miss him.

Twelve o'clock came and went. Jackie glanced at his watch anxiously, and watched the street for any sign of her. Had she changed her mind? Or had she perhaps somehow realized that they had set a trap for her?

He was almost happy to see her a moment later. She was in a Cadillac convertible driven by

Jay. They came to an abrupt stop at the curb, almost directly in front of him, and honked the horn. Jackie picked up his suitcase and walked hurriedly toward them. He resisted an impulse to glance in Rich's direction. A single glance might make his enemies suspicious. At any rate, he had no doubts regarding Rich. His fellow agent was sure to be watching, and understanding the meeting.

Anna opened the door as be neared, and reached out for the suitcase. "Is it all here?" she asked, closing the door again.

"Every cent," he assured her. "That takes care of my end of the bargain. How soon will I get Sophie back?"

"I'll let you know," she told him. Before Jackie could question them further, she had signaled to Jay, and the car pulled quickly away from him. Jackie remained where he was for a few minutes, lest they look back to observe his actions. From the corner of his, eye, however, he saw Rich's car pull out from its parking place and move off down the street after them.

When both cars were out of sight, Jackie turned and ran to his own car, a block away. As he started up the powerful engine, he switched on the radio.

"Still with them?" he asked.

"No problems," Rich's voice assured him. "They don't even suspect they're being followed. Apparently it never occurred to them you might have a partner."

"Good, keep with them, but not so close that they'll see you and become suspicious. I'm right behind you."

Rich gave him directions, street by street. Anna and Jay were taking a roundabout route, changing directions often, but they remained apparently unaware of the fact that they were being followed. At Rich's directions, Jackie followed the same route. They were moving slowly back into the Silverlake area. Probably, he concluded, they had a house somewhere in the neighborhood of the previous one.

"I think they're almost there," Rich said finally. "They turned down a dead end street. Wait where you are. I'll park and go for a stroll."

Jackie pulled to the curb, engine running, and waited impatiently. In a few minutes, Rich's voice came to him again. "Okay, I've seen the house," he said. "I'll wait here until you join me."

Jackie started up again. A few blocks later, he pulled up behind Rich's car. His brawny friend came back and joined him in his car.

"It's at the end of that street," Rich explained, indicating the corner just ahead. "An old house, set back by itself."

"What about getting in?"

"We can do that from the back, the way I see it. This area is all hills. There's an empty house behind them, with a yard that's terraced down to theirs, and there's plenty of trees and bushes. With any kind of luck, they won't see us approaching."

"That only leaves the question of getting inside the house itself," Jackie said. "We'll have to cross that, bridge when we get to it."

They started off together, going past the street on which the dognapper's house was located. At the next corner, Rich turned, leading the way. At the end of the block, Jackie saw the empty house Rich had described, its windows bare, yard untended. There were FOR RENT signs in the windows and on stakes in the yard.

"If anyone sees us, they'll think we're planning to rent this place," Rich said, indicating the signs.

They walked about the house, studying it as though they were genuinely interested in it, slowly making their way to the rear. When they were out of sight of the street, they abandoned the pretense.

"That's their house," Rich said, pointing toward the rear of the property.

Jackie could just see the roof of the house Rich indicated, jutting above the hilly grounds on which they presently stood. Rich was right; the terraced grounds, and the untended growth of shrubs and trees, provided them with a natural cover. He led the way quickly in that direction.

From the last terrace, the ground sloped sharply downward, to end at a fence and a row of bushes that separated this property from the next. They scurried quickly down the hill, once again protecting themselves from sight by the bushes.

Moving stealthily and without conversation, they crept along the bushes until Jackie spotted a break in the fence. He signaled Rich, and then dropped to the ground, inching his way through the shrubbery on his stomach.

Halfway through the fence, he paused. From here on in, it would be touch and go. Once they emerged from the shrubbery, they would be visible to anyone watching from the house. He took a deep breath, pulled himself the rest of the way through, and sprinted toward the house. Reaching it, he flattened himself against the wall, and waited for Rich to join him.

So far there was nothing to indicate that they had been spotted. He glanced around. From here, they could not be observed by any bewildered neighbors. It was a perfect place to use the "stopper", a psychological weapon he used only in drastic situations.

First Jackie bent down and slipped off his shoes. He twisted the sole of one, revealing a secret compartment, from which he removed a thin but deadly throwing knife. Setting the shoes on the ground, he peeled off his socks too.

Rich grinned as he realized what his friend was up to. Jackie quickly unfastened his belt and slipped his trousers down, stepping out of them and folding them neatly before he deposited them with his shoes.

With a shrug, Rich began also to undress. A few minutes later, both of them were nude from their waists down, their shoes, socks, trousers and underwear neatly stacked beside the house. Rich winced as he stooped to add the last item to his stack and his overly generous sexual endowments dragged across the rough ground. The "stopper" had certain disadvantages for someone of his proportions, he thought as he straightened up, rubbing the heavy hung but bruised area.

It was a peculiar sight, and for that reason, an effective one in dealing with criminals, particularly in a situation such as this one. They had no way of knowing what they were walking into. Their enemies might be waiting, weapons ready. Jackie had found that the "stopper" never failed to give him an advantage. The shock of seeing someone suddenly burst into a room, naked from the waist down, usually gave him a precious few seconds to move before his opponents recovered and sprang into action.

This time the shock would be a double one, and he was particularly glad that Rich was with him. He was confident that a glimpse of Rich from the waist down would be sufficient to temporarily stun just about anyone.

They moved carefully along the wall. In his hand Jackie held the throwing knife. He had given the gun to Rich. Alert for any sound or movement, they reached the door.

They froze there, listening. From inside they could hear the sound of voices. The dognappers were together, talking. It was Jackie's guess that this door opened directly into the kitchen. Grimly, he gave Rich the signal. He reached for the door, turning the knob with a painfully slow movement. It yielded. The door was unlocked. Careful not to warn his prey by making a sound, Jackie twisted the knob until the latch gave. He took a deep breath, and yanked the door open. Together, the two of them sprang into the room.

The "stopper" worked with its customary success. He had been right in guessing the room to be the kitchen. Jay, Anna, and the other man were seated at the round kitchen table, arguing over their coffee. They looked up as the door was thrown open, and froze at the sight.

The ugly bruiser with no name recovered first. His hand went to his pocket, but before he could fully draw the gun, Rich's bullet had winged him. The man clutched his arm with a yelp of pain.

Jay literally dived across the table. The light flickered on the blade of the knife he held, but Jackie's knife was faster, however. Jay screamed too as the thin blade slashed through his hand.

Jackie moved toward Anna, but she was not so easily caught. With a sudden movement she threw her scalding hot coffee into his face. Jackie stumbled backward, temporarily blinded by the steaming liquid. It gave Anna the second she needed to dart from the room through the swinging door opposite them.

"Are you all right?" Rich asked, whirling Jackie about.

Jackie ran a hand across his face, clearing his eyes. "Never mind me," he cried. "Stop her before she reaches, Sophie."

Together they dashed after Anna. They burst into the adjoining room, but they were already too late. Across the room from them, Anna held Sophie, still unconscious, in her arms. The blade of a knife was pressed against Sophie's throat.

"One move and the dog dies," she shouted as they entered the room.

THE MAN FROM C.A.M.P.

♠ CHAPTER ELEVEN ♠
λ

Jackie and Rich froze in their tracks. The distance across the room was too great. They could not cross it in time to prevent Anna from carrying out her threat.

Her companions burst into the room behind them. Seeing Anna in control of the situation, their consternation turned to triumph.

"Well, well, looks like pretty boy has been outfoxed again," Jay crowed, holding his injured hand. "And this time we're going to settle a few scores."

"I'd like to tear them apart with my bare hands," the other one snarled. It was plain, however, that he was unlikely to carry out that threat. One arm was still bandaged from the wound Jackie had inflicted in their previous encounter, and his other arm was now wounded as well, by Rich's shot a few seconds before.

"It'll be a while before you're in shape to tear any one apart," Jackie informed him.

The man snarled again and attempted a threatening gesture. The effort only caused him to grimace in pain.

"I got to see a doctor," he informed Anna

"Don't be a fool," she snapped. "We can't take you to a doctor with gunshot wounds. The doctor would call in the police immediately, and then where would we be?"

Jay had gone to the kitchen to retrieve the gun. He frowned thoughtfully as he returned. "Come to think of it," he said to Anna. "He's not gonna be much help to us for quite a while."

Anna smiled wickedly as the meaning of his comment became clear. "Yes, you're right. In fact, he would only be a hindrance to us."

Their companion was slower to understand. Finally he began to see what they were driving at. Astonishment and disbelief passed across his face, to be replaced by anger.

"Oh no, you don't," he growled, advancing menacingly toward Anna. "You two ain't cuttin' me out...."

The gun in Jay's hand roared. The wounded man jerked as the bullet struck. Then, disbelief again written on his face, he turned and managed to stumble in the direction of his assailant. He got two steps before he fell to the floor.

"You monsters," Jackie gasped as the horrible drama was enacted before his eyes. Like the beasts they were, they were turning now upon one another, destroying their own kind. But unless he could come up with something, they would destroy him and Rich as well.

144

Jay turned to him, the gun aimed at his stomach. "You're next," he said with a fiendish grin. Jackie prepared himself for the bullet. Beside him, he felt, Rich tense.

"No, wait," Anna ordered. "I have a better idea for these two. Why not turn them over to our friends in the basement?"

Although the meaning of the statement was not clear to Jackie, it was obviously one that pleased Jay. His eyes gleamed brightly, and he smiled his agreement.

"Yeah, that should be an interesting experience," he said.

"This way," Anna ordered Jackie and Rich, indicating the hall beyond the room they were in. With Jay and the gun, behind them, Jackie and Rich followed Anna down the hallway. She opened a door, revealing a steep, narrow flight of steps going downward.

"After you," she told them, with a wave of her hand.

Jackie led the way down the steps, into the dim, musty basement. For a moment he did not recognize the figure lying on the floor, hands and feet tied. As his eyes became accustomed to the light, he gasped in astonishment.

"Agatha!" he cried.

"Jackie, thank God it's you." Lady Agatha's voice was faint, and he appeared barely conscious.

"I thought you'd enjoy that little surprise," Anna said from behind Jackie. "And don't get your hopes up, Agatha dear, he's in just as bad a spot as you."

"What are you doing with him here?" Rich demanded angrily.

"He was getting a little nosy," Jay explained. "So Don brought him here. We were going to give him a really exciting send off. But now that you two are here, you can share in the fun."

They had reached the bottom of the steps. Jackie's attention had been riveted on Agatha and he had failed to see the large cage that occupied nearly one half of the basement. As he came nearer, however, he heard a menacing growl. He turned in that direction and his breath caught in his throat. There, behind the bars that separated them from the rest of the room, were six of the most vicious creatures he had ever seen, Doberman Pincers—even at their best, the breed was a dangerous one. But these animals were like wild beasts. Aroused by the disturbance, they sprang to life, jumping at the bars and barking and snarling in fury. Jackie needed no one to tell him that these dogs were deadly.

"They've been trained to kill, too," Anna said proudly. "And I've added to their tempers by starving them the last day or so. Of course, the fact that Jay beats them regularly with a whip hasn't made them very docile either."

"They'd tear a man to ribbons," Rich said, staring in fascination at the terrifying beasts. On the floor, Agatha cringed each time the dogs leaped against the bars.

"That's just what they've planned," Agatha said hoarsely. "They've been telling me that when they were ready to leave, they'd turn those creatures loose on me."

146

"That's exactly what we plan to do," Anna agreed. "Except that now there'll be three of you to share the fun."

"That's the most dreadful thing I've ever heard of," Jackie protested. "Is there no heart within that beautiful body of yours?"

"Sure, it's made of hand tooled leather." She laughed loudly at her little joke, then grew serious again as she turned to Jay. "Mark should be back in a few minutes with those plane tickets. We'd better be getting ourselves ready."

"Just to be on the safe side," Jay said, "I think that we should tie up these two."

"Good idea," she agreed. "The little blond is a bit too resourceful for his own good—or ours."

While Anna, held the gun on them, Jay found some rope and quickly tied Jackie's hands behind his back. Then, throwing him roughly to the floor, he tied his feet also. Rich was next. In minutes both of them were prone on the floor, helplessly bound.

"As for your precious dog," Anna declared, "you wanted her so badly, I'll give you your wish. She can die with you in this room."

She dropped the still sleeping Sophie on the floor beside them and started toward the stairs.

"Unlock the gate to the kennel," she instructed Jay as she mounted the steps.

They'll tear me apart too," he protested, alarmed by the command. "You know how they hate me."

"Don't be silly. It will take them a few minutes to discover that the gate is unlatched. Just slip the bolt and make a dash for the steps."

As for herself, Anna was plainly taking no chances. While she was giving her orders, she had continued up the steps to the top. Without waiting for further protest on Jay's part, she started through the door.

"Can we spare a few minutes?" Jay called after her. He had glanced down, his gaze resting on Jackie's semi-nude body. His tongue darted over his lips,

"For what?"

"I just remembered, I got a little score to settle with our friend here." He grinned broadly.

"Fine. Just don't be too long," she decided. "I want to leave as soon as Mark gets back."

The door closed after her. Still licking his lips, Jay turned back to Jackie. His eyes were devouring the naked lower portion of Jackie's torso.

"Seems to me," he said, starting to unbuckle his belt. "The last time you and I got together with our pants off, you gave me a pretty rough time."

"You had it coming," Jackie snapped.

"Yeah? Maybe you do too."

As they talked, Jay had slipped his trousers down. Beneath them, he was nude, and the heavy hanging endowments thus revealed were as monstrously huge as Jackie had remembered. He shuddered as he thought of what was in store for him.

Jay kicked off his shoes and stepped out of his pants. As he toyed briefly with himself, his eyes still upon Jackie's bare bottom, his flesh began to swell, assuming dreadful proportions.

"If you touch him," Rich growled, struggling against the ropes that held him, "I'll...."

"You'll what?" Jay turned in Rich's direction. He paused to study the view he had of Rich. "As a matter of fact, I may get around to you too."

Jackie saw the look of frustration on Rich's face. He knew that what Jay intended was a form of activity to which Rich was not very accustomed. For himself, accommodating Jay would be an agonizing ordeal. For Rich, he knew it would be infinitely worse.

"Leave him alone," Jackie said. "Do what you want with me. That should satisfy your vile lust."

Jay only laughed again. "How touching," he said. He was ready now for his attack. Stooping down, he roughly turned Jackie over on his stomach. The bare cement of the floor scraped painfully across Jackie's skin. The weight of Jay's body, literally thrown over his, nearly crushed him. He winced as he felt the first probing at his backside. There would be no mercy shown to him, he was certain of that. The force being exerted was tremendous as his attacker sought an entrance. Jackie bit his lips as he felt his flesh yielding to the mammoth demands. He felt as though his body were being split asunder.

He closed his eyes, forcing his thoughts elsewhere, away from the invasion that was slowly but surely taking place. The searing pain inched deeper and deeper. It would have been easier, he knew, had he been able to change his position, but he knew such a request would only be denied him.

There seemed no end to the ordeal. With each vicious thrust, be felt he could surely not endure more. Jay's hands gripped his naked hips tightly, the nails cutting into his flesh. Jackie breathed in gasps, scarcely able to contain the groans that formed in his throat.

Over him, Jay was panting hoarsely in his ear. Jackie knew it must be an ordeal for him as well, but he was deriving pleasure from the pain he knew he was inflicting.

"Yell, damn you," Jay hissed in frustration. "Why don't you yell?"

Jackie remained silent, refusing to give his attacker that satisfaction, which only added to Jay's fury. His attack grew more frenzied, more brutal. He threw himself against Jackie with such force that Jackie was again and again crushed into the rough cement.

Mercifully the act was brief. Jackie recognized the telltale signs of Jay's approaching climax, and knew that he would not have to endure the slipping, sliding torture much longer. There were hoarse cries in his ear, and a final blow that seemed to split him asunder, and, at last, the hot convulsive spasms that told him the end had been reached.

Jay lay over him, pinning him to the floor for several seconds more. Then, abruptly, he withdrew and stood up. He stared down at Jackie for a moment; then, in anger because he had elicited no yells of pain, delivered a bone jarring kick to Jackie's ass.

Jackie was grateful for one fact, however. In reaching his orgasm, Jay had temporarily lost his desire, and his capability, for defiling Rich. With an angry frown in Rich's direction, Jay donned his trousers again.

Now that his grudge had been settled, Jay returned his attention to the dogs in the cage. It was plain that he was less than enthusiastic about the chore that had been assigned to him by Anna, the task of releasing the animals from their cage. He approached the cage cautiously. At the sight of him, the dogs again renewed their attack at the bars, and Jay stepped fearfully back.

"Why don't you offer them some of that limp meat you like to throw around?" Jackie asked with a bitchy smile.

"Shut up," Jay snarled, but there was more fear in his voice than anger.

The door at the top of the steps opened, and Anna appeared. "Aren't you finished yet? Mark just pulled into the drive. We have lots to get done."

"Okay, okay," he snapped. "Leave the door open."

When she had gone, he summoned his courage and again approached the cage, faltering slightly when the uproar within the cage started again.

He looked around and saw a small stone lying on the floor. Picking that up, he threw it into the cage, so that it landed on the far side from the gate. The dogs, in hope that this might be a morsel of food, dashed in that direction. With a swift movement, Jay threw the bolt and, without pause, turned and raced for the steps. He was through it, and the door closed, before the dogs had abandoned their examination of the stone.

Anna had been right: for the moment, the dogs were unaware that the gate was unlatched.

At the top, Jay paused too. "Have fun," he called down to them. "I'll peek in later, just to see how the party is going." With that he closed and locked the door.

Jackie and Rich exchanged anxious glances. This was a tight situation, as dangerous as any they had ever been in before.

"We've got to get out of these ropes," Jackie said. As he made the statement, he was scooting across the floor toward Rich.

"Turn yourself around," Rich said. "I'll try to work your hands free."

It was difficult moving about, tied as they were. It seemed an eternity before Jackie had managed to scoot himself about on the rough cement floor. At last, with a wave of relief, he felt Rich's fingers at his wrist. He moved an inch further, and his hands were within Rich's grasp.

It was a slow and laborious effort. With his own hands tied, and behind him where he could not see what he was doing, Rich's efforts were sorely hampered. Time and again he lost his grip on the ropes holding Jackie's wrists.

"I think it's coming," he gasped finally. "A few more minutes will do it."

They were lying back to back, with the result that Rich was turned away from the cage. He could not see what Jackie could see. As Jackie watched with anxious eyes, one of the dogs brushed against the door of the cage. It swung open slightly.

"We may not have a few minutes," Jackie said tensely. His eyes swept around the room, seeking some hope of escape. Near him on the floor, Sophie stirred slightly, at last beginning to regain consciousness as the effects of the drug wore off.

"Sophie!" Jackie called her name sharply. He could almost see the struggle within her, between the clinging effects of the drug, and her instinctive reaction to his call. He called her name again, loudly and sharply.

She stirred again, feebly. Her eyes opened and she peered about in bewilderment. Then, after a few seconds, she attempted to scramble to her feet. The first effort was a failure. She tried again, and this time managed, to stand. With clumsy, labored movements, she came toward Jackie.

The movements, and the sound, however, had attracted the attention of the beasts in the cage. One of them jumped, and struck the door. It creaked noisily open, and the Pincer was out of the cage. For a moment he seemed not to comprehend what had happened, staring curiously about him.

Jackie's heart seemed to stop in his chest. The other dogs approached the opening, sniffing suspiciously. Then, still sniffing, they advanced out of the cage also.

Sophie had reached Jackie, and licked his face feebly. She was still weak and dazed, more asleep than awake—but she was the only thing that stood between them and death from the six beasts that had clustered together for a moment.

With a menacing growl that left little doubt of his intentions, the leader of the pack began to move slowly toward them, his teeth bared, his ears laid back.

For a second it seemed all was lost. Sophie seemed oblivious to the approaching danger. Then, at last, her battle instincts returned to her. She sniffed, her eyes narrowing, and turned, to see the animals creeping near.

At Sophie's warning growl, the leader of the pack hesitated for an instant. Then, with his teeth gleaming savagely, he lunged forward.

"Sophie, kill!" Jackie shouted frantically, straining his wrists against the ropes that still held him. Unless Sophie, still groggy from the drugs that had been used to render her unconscious, could hold off the six raging beasts, they would not live long enough to free themselves.

♠ <u>CHAPTER TWELVE</u> ♠
λ

Sophie met the attack with a fury that equaled that of the maddened beasts. Two bodies crashed together, and they fell to the floor, sprawling. The teeth of the Doberman tore the skin at Sophie's shoulder, but he had missed the throat he had aimed for, and he was never to have a second chance. Sophie's own razor sharp teeth sank into his throat, and she threw her head mightily from side to side as the Doberman thrashed and kicked.

The others were upon her then. Jackie watched in horror as teeth flashed, bodies grappled and collided. Just when Sophie's doom seemed certain, he felt the ropes at his wrists give. With all the strength he could summon, he yanked. The last, of the bonds gave, and his hands were free.

He had decided already upon his only hope. There was no time to untie his feet. He thrust his hand into the pocket of the jacket he still wore. His memory had served him right: his lighter was still there.

As he flicked the lighter, he threw himself forward, toward the stack of newspapers and debris nearby. The paper caught fire, the single flame suddenly blazing brilliantly.

Even as he turned, Jackie lifted the blazing papers and hurled them into the midst of the fighting animals. There were yelps of fear as the dogs leaped back away from their greatest dread, fire.

"Sophie, here," Jackie called, frantically setting another paper afire. For a second he thought he was too late. The other dogs had leaped back, but Sophie lay where she had fallen in the battle. Then, with a feeble shake of her head, she rose and ran, limping, toward him.

The sight of their adversary, and the fact that the fire had nearly burned out, gave the Pincers new courage. They moved to follow, but Jackie waited until Sophie was almost to him, then he threw the second blazing paper, between Sophie and the Pincers. They stopped short, howling, in frustration as she made her temporary escape into Jackie's arms.

There was no time for reunions, however. Jackie threw all of the papers into the blaze, creating a small barrier of fire. It would last only briefly. Every second was precious. He turned to Rich, and worked feverishly to untie Rich's hands, then Agatha's. The three of them tore at the ropes at their feet.

The fire was nearly gone, and there was only one newspaper left. Jumping to his feet, Jackie wadded it tightly into a torch, and held it into the fire.

"The steps," he ordered the others, holding the torch between them and the enraged Pincers.

Rich and Agatha scrambled to the steps and up them. Jackie followed, holding the dogs at bay with the flaming paper. It was burning down quickly, however. A few more seconds, and they would be defenseless.

Rich had almost reached the door at the top when they heard the sound of the key in the lock. He froze in his tracks as the door opened, and Jay appeared.

For a second, Jay stood in bewilderment. The scene was clearly not what he had expected to see. Then, abruptly, he attempted to slam the door, but Rich was faster. The two struggled desperately for seconds. With a mighty lunge, Jay pulled himself free from Rich's grip, but the effort had thrown him off balance. He stumbled backward, lost his footing, and toppled down the stairs.

Jackie grabbed frantically for him, trying to arrest the fall, but Jay's shirt tore away in his fingers, and Jay hurtled to the bottom, right into the faces of the dog pack.

There was a scream of terror, and a roar of triumph from the dogs. They forgot the other humans, turning their madness against the man whom they so hated, the one who had starved and beaten them.

Rich moved down the steps, but Jackie caught his arm. "It's too late," he cried. Even from here, he could see them tear at Jay's throat. His limp body was, as he himself had described it, being torn to ribbons.

The three of them and Sophie dashed through the door, slamming it after them. As they burst into the hallway, Anna and Mark Harris ran from the other room.

"Jay, what is it?" Anna called. She stopped, the words caught in her throat, as she saw the three of them before her.

Rich dived from where he was, catching Harris in a flying tackle that in itself was nearly enough to render the man unconscious.

Anna turned to run, but Jackie dashed to her, catching her in a violent grip. She struggled with the strength of a wildcat, hissing and cursing. Jackie realized too late that she was wearing her gloves, with the steel claws in them. They slashed across his arm, ripping the flesh. With a cry of pain, he instinctively released his grip. She jerked away from him, and raised a hand to bring the claws down across his face.

Agatha was there before she could strike, however. Anna's sleek, long hair was suddenly caught in an angry grasp, and yanked violently backward. With a yell, Anna staggered and fell backward. Before she could recover, they had her firmly in their power, each of them holding an arm.

"You've nothing on me," she howled. "You can't hold me."

"Don't kid yourself," Jackie replied calmly. "We've plenty of evidence now regarding the dognapping, not to mention kidnapping Agatha. And you're forgetting we saw Jay murder your cohort in cold blood, and the fact that you tried to kill us all. For the next few years, you're going to be the one in a cage."

* * * * * * *

158

It took a considerable amount of time to clean things up. The police came, in the person of Jackie's old friend Inspector Abernathy, and Anna and Mark were carried away to face the consequences of their horrible crimes. In another room of the house, they found the collection of dogs that the group had stolen. Jackie volunteered the services of C.A.M.P. in locating the owners of the animals, and at a call from Rich, a special van arrived from High Camp to deliver the animals temporarily to C.A.M.P.'s own state of the art kennels.

A special police crew arrived to deal with the vicious Dobermans in the basement. Gas was used to knock them out, and Jackie could not help his sadness at the knowledge that the animals would undoubtedly be put to death.

"They too were victims of this unscrupulous band," he said sadly. "Driven mad, turned into savages. The crimes of Anna Lingus and her friends were many."

At last it was ended. Jackie, Rich, and Agatha prepared to leave the house. They had reached the front door when Agatha stopped and giggled.

"I think you two are forgetting something," he said.

At first Jackie and Rich were both puzzled; then following Agatha's glance, they looked down. In all the activity, they had forgotten that they were both still naked from their waists down.

"I thought that one policeman was being overly friendly," Rich commented with a laugh.

They went back through the house, toward the rear where they had left their clothes. As they passed by one of the closets, Jackie heard a faint whimpering sound. He stopped, and swung the half-closed door open.

Inside, huddled far back in a corner, was a tiny white poodle, scarcely more than a puppy. At first he cringed away from Jackie, sniffing suspiciously. Jackie knelt and reached out to pat the tiny white head.

Sophie, too, made a brief examination, sniffing curiously but in a friendly manner. At last the puppy decided that these strangers were friends. The tail moved shyly, and he licked Jackie's hand with a warm tongue.

Jackie gathered him into his arms and lifted him from the closet. In the light, he could see a note attached to the poodle's collar. He removed it, and handed it to Rich to read.

"Anna," Rich read aloud. "The old guy we stole this one from has kicked the bucket. He has no family, so we aren't going to get a reward out of this mutt. May as well get rid of it.

"It's signed 'Don'," he finished.

"Somehow this little thing must have escaped from the room in which they kept the dogs," Jackie mused, "before they could 'get rid of it,' and he hid in here."

"I suppose we could find a home for him someplace," Rich said. "He doesn't look like a prize dog, but he's cute enough."

"As far as that goes," Agatha commented, "I could take him myself. I think he's adorable."

Jackie was thoughtful for a moment. "No, I think I know just what to do with this one," he said finally. He glanced at his two companions with a smile. "How do you two feel about strip shows?"

"Seeing or giving?" Agatha asked suspiciously.

"Salvaging," was Jackie's reply. With his two friends giving him puzzled looks, he led the way from the house.

When he and Rich had dressed, they made their way to Jackie's car.

"Where to?" Rich asked, having been elected to drive.

"First, I want to stop by Paulette's club, and visit with her for a few minutes."

"Paulette?" Agatha remained puzzled. "I don't get this. You know Paulette has high-class entertainment at the Casa Gee. She doesn't hire strippers."

Jackie said nothing. They drove across town, to the small, very chic nightclub owned by his old friend, Paulette. It was, as they all knew, the 'in' spot of the city, and anyone who was anyone in the city knew Paulette, by her first name. She had started in vaudeville, as a child performer. There had been an unsuccessful attempt, as an adult, to go into movies. Fortunately, the stormy blonde had been wise enough to know that her appeal was to a small, and live, audience.

Instead of movies, she had started playing clubs, with increasing success, until she had opened this one of her own. Here she occasionally performed herself, but more often the stage of the Casa Gee was a showcase for the most brilliant new talent in the entertainment world. Many a successful career had been launched under her auspices, and producers and entrepreneurs the world over regularly came to look over the show.

Their visit there was brief, and by the time they continued on their way, Rich and Agatha were no longer puzzled, but were as excited as Jackie.

* * * * * * *

As usual, it was Fury Fan who met them at the door of her apartment. She beamed when she saw Jackie, shook hands warmly with Agatha when introduced, and gaped in amusement when she got a good look at Rich.

"Hey, O. K.," she yelled into the apartment. "Get off the john and come look at this. I haven't seen so much man in one spot since we did that benefit at the Marine camp."

O. K. was no less impressed than Fury had been. While Rich blushed furiously, the aged redhead's eyes devoured the many inches of his brawny body.

"Gawd," she gasped, clutching her bosom. "I think I just broke a mainspring."

Jackie's laugh was interrupted by a sharp bark from under his jacket.

"What's this, a wind up toy?" Fury asked as Jackie brought the puppy into view. Sophie, at Jackie's feet, exchanged friendly barks with the little one.

"It was sort of a leftover from the dognapping case," Jackie said. He explained the outcome of the case, a task that took considerable time due to the frequent interruptions of the two women.

"Damn, I'd like to have gotten my hands into that witch's hair," Fury said when she heard of the final fight, and Agatha's part in it. "I hope you pulled it gray."

"I was an Olympic finalist in hair pulling," Agatha answered. "It'll be a few weeks before she gets her eyes uncrossed."

"Anyway," Jackie concluded. "We're stuck with this little thing. Our only hope is in finding a home for him."

Fury sniffed faintly, casting a glance at the puppy in Jackie's arms. "Well, if O. K. didn't eat like a horse, I wouldn't mind having another pet around here. But I don't suppose we'd make a very desirable home for such a little tyke."

"Me?" O. K. was appropriately indignant. "We could always give the pup your dinner. You could live a year on that blubber of yours."

She turned to Jackie. "Pay no mind to this old bag. We'd both love a dog like that, and you know it as well as she does."

"He's yours, then," Jackie answered, handing the puppy into O. K.'s arms. The ex-stripper hugged it happily, to be rewarded by having her face licked enthusiastically.

"Don't wear it out," Fury protested. "Let me show you how to hold a dog."

The question of a home for the orphan poodle seemed definitely settled. Nor did Jackie doubt for a moment that it would be a happy home, one filled with tender care and much affection.

Fury smiled at Jackie with tears in her eyes. "Look, there isn't much we can do to pay you back. But there's one thing we still got, and that's our talent. If you still want to see a performance, I know two old bags that are ready to put on a show any-time."

"As a matter of fact," Jackie replied, winking in the direction of Rich and Agatha. "That's what I wanted to see you about. We need a favor. Or rather, a friend of ours does. She has a club, a small one, mind you, and she's in a pinch. The entertain-ers she had walked out on her, and she needs some-one to fill in. Think you'd be interested?"

The two women exchanged uncertain glances. "I don't know," Fury said finally, in a timid voice. "We ain't kids any more, you know. If it was just a show for you guys, that's one thing, but a club... gee, we ain't got much left in the looks department, or voice either."

"Well, in your years in the business, you must have accumulated a bit of material," Jackie argued.

"She's got more material than most of these dames performing today will ever dream of," O. K. said. "Jokes, songs, dance routines, you name it. And costumes, too. Let me tell you, the two of us still got every costume we ever used, and every prop."

"And I'll bet you know how to play to an au-dience, too," Jackie encouraged them eagerly.

"Sure, damned right," Fury agreed. "Neither one of us ever played to an audience but what we couldn't have them eating out of our hands."

"I played the Palace once," O. K. added. "Same bill as Harry Lauder."

"We still do things together," Fury said, her instinctive pride replacing her uncertainty. "Just around the place, for our own pleasure, you under-

164

stand. Worked out some great routines, if I must say so."

Jackie was beaming. He knew that the two of them would end up winning the argument for him.

* * * * * * *

The audience was a little cold at first. From the ringside table Paulette had provided them, Jackie and Rich waited anxiously for the show to get under way. He knew many of the people had come expecting to see a group of performers who were rapidly earning names for themselves, and had been scheduled to appear on this particular evening. The switch had been made without any previous announcement.

The two strippers came on together, two aging women who, at first sight and even first sound, seemed to have little to offer in the way of entertainment value. Jackie watched tensely, sharing the nervousness he was sure they felt. But if Fury Fan and O. K. Plenty, billed as the Dowager Queens of Burlesque, were nervous, they didn't show it. They seemed, from the moment they stepped on stage, to have come home, to have entered the world in which they belonged. And by the time they had finished their first little skit, the audience knew it too. The applause, faint and spotty when they had been introduced, grew warmer, and more enthusiastic.

It was a nostalgic show, reminiscent of the best of burlesque and vaudeville. Old or not, it was quite clear that these two had known the best of both—had known it, and knew how to bring it briefly to life again for this audience, many of whom dated from the same era.

They talked, and joked, and even danced a little. They sang songs, some of them timeless hits, others clever numbers they had presumably invented themselves: "The Man in The Moon Is a Fairy;" "Everybody Loves My Body," and many others. The audience listened, laughed, occasionally brushed away a tear, and even hummed along on some of the songs.

And finally, with surprisingly little effort, Fury hoisted her considerable weight onto the piano at which O. K. was seated. A hush fell over the audience as Fury began her song: "Love For Sale". Neither she nor her voice were pretty, but all of the magic that Jackie had detected before was in evidence. It was the delivery of a star.

The applause when she finished was literally deafening. The stage had gone dark, and Rich turned from it, thinking that the show was finished.

"There's more," Jackie informed him. "They've still got a number with their partner."

"I didn't know they'd taken on a partner," Rich turned back to the stage as the lights came up again.

"Just for tonight, command performance," Jackie explained.

At first it was difficult to recognize the third figure on the stage. Covered with spangles and plumes, replete with blonde wig, she appeared to be another great from the world of burlesque.

"My God," Rich exclaimed finally. "It's Lady Agatha, in drag!"

The trio on stage danced and sang their way through a rousing arrangement of "We Three," and it was plain that all three were having the time of their lives.

As the number ended to another roar of applause, Jackie heard a faint buzzing from his watch, a signal that C.A.M.P. was again in need of his services.

"It's C.A.M.P.," he whispered, nudging Rich.

"It certainly is," Rich agreed absentmindedly, still clapping loudly. "It's the campiest."

♠ ABOUT THE AUTHOR ♠
λ

Lecturer, former writing instructor and early rab-
ble-rouser for gay rights and freedom of the press,
VICTOR J. BANIS *is the critically acclaimed author*
("...a master storyteller"—Publishers Weekly) *of*
more than 140 published novels and nonfiction
works, and his verse and short pieces have ap-
*peared in numerous journals (*Blithe House Quar-
terly, *Fall 2006) and anthologies (*Charmed Lives,
Lethe Press, 2006).